FROM ABOVE... WITH LOVE

FROM ABOVE... WITH LOVE

ANDREW MATTHEWS

RED FOX

A RED FOX BOOK : 009943427X

First published in Great Britain by Red Fox 2002
an imprint of Random House Children's Books

1 3 5 7 9 10 8 6 4 2

Text copyright © Andrew Matthews 2002
Cover illustration copyright © Nick Sharratt 2002

The right of Andrew Matthews to be identified as the author of this work
has been asserted by him in accordance with the Copyright, Designs and
Patents Act 1988

Papers used by Random House Children's Books are natural, recyclable
products made from wood grown in sustainable forests. The
manufacturing processes conform to the environmental regulations of the
country of origin.

Red Fox Books are published by Random House Children's Books,
61-63 Uxbridge Road, London W5 5SA,
a division of The Random House Group Ltd,
in Australia by Random House Australia (Pty) Ltd,
20 Alfred Street, Milsons Point, Sydney, NSW 2061, Australia,
in New Zealand by Random House New Zealand Ltd,
18 Poland Road, Glenfield, Auckland 10, New Zealand,
and in South Africa by Random House (Pty) Ltd,
Endulini, 5A Jubilee Road, Parktown 2193, South Africa

THE RANDOM HOUSE GROUP Limited Reg. No. 954009
www.randomhouse.co.uk

A CIP catalogue record for this book is available from the British Library.

Printed and bound in Great Britain by
Bookmarque Ltd, Croydon, Surrey.

for Jenny, my Engine,
with lots and lots of love
(but in a nice way)

'Every visible thing in this world
is put under the charge of an angel.'

St Augustine

1

If they ever make a movie of this, I know just how it will start. The camera is looking down on an open-air market at the edge of a private airfield. It's a late afternoon in winter. The trees on the horizon have no leaves, the sky is overcast and everything's grey – except the market. The stalls have been strung with coloured lights and a PA system is churning out Christmas songs.

Now the camera goes into the crowd at eye level and moves around, checking out what's on offer. You've got your cheese stall, CD stall, trainers stall; you've got fruit and veg, meat, stereo systems, ornaments, clothes and the latest kid's craze – a merry, festive, robot-dinosaur death-ray toy.

The camera stops at one stall. It sells fibre-optic lamps that look like alien plants. There are two people behind the stall. One is a grumpy middle-aged guy in a balaclava helmet; the other is a girl. The girl's sixteen, wears faded denim jeans and a black leather jacket. She's tall, lanky, flat-chested, her mousey hair is scraped back into a manky hair-tie, her grey eyes are watery and her nose is red. From the expression on her face, you can tell that she doesn't want to be where she is, because it's cold and boring, but it's a job and she needs the money.

Take a long look at her. Not much of a heroine, is she? No blonde hair, cornflower-blue eyes or peaches-and-cream complexion. Her chin is too pointed, the bits between her eyelids and her eyebrows are too fat, the mark on her left cheek might be a ripening zit and she's *way* too skinny. The most interesting thing about her is that she's ignorant – not dumb, but ignorant about what's going to happen to her. Her little world is about to get seriously weird, but she has no idea. She thinks it's a normal, late Saturday afternoon close to Christmas – the poor shmuck!

She's me: I'm Lauren.

2

You think Christmas is a time of peace on Earth and goodwill unto all men? Let the door hit your butt on the way out. Christmas is the pits. Saturday trade has been picking up as Christmas gets nearer, and today it's mayhem. The punters are scuttling round like ants whose nest has just been dug up. They're stressed-out and frantic. They're bad-tempered, hassled and they're buying the most amazing tack. Would you believe that the guy selling plastic reindeer, with red noses that light up, ran out of stock and packed up two hours ago? People are buying anything; anything except fibre-optic lamps, that is. We haven't done any business since lunch.

I turn to Mr Fairbrother (the grouch in the balaclava) and say, 'Not much doing, is there? Shall I start clearing away?'

Mr Fairbrother looks at me like I've offered to extract his wisdom teeth without anaesthetic. 'The market closes at half four,' he says. 'I don't pay people for doing nothing.'

He can say that again. I have to be at the market by seven a.m. and if I'm late Mr

Fairbrother docks my wages. This job wasn't my idea. My parents thought it would be good for me, that it would teach me the value of money, and blah. What it's taught me is that Mr Fairbrother is a sour-faced slave driver. I'm not employed, I'm exploited.

Customer alert! A woman wanders over to the stall and starts handling the merchandise. She looks at me and says, 'What are they?'

'Lamps,' I say, with my most winning smile.

'Lamps? They don't give off much light, do they?'

'They're not supposed to,' I explain. 'You look at them while the colours change. They're very popular. All my friends have got them. I've got three.'

I'm lying. My friends wouldn't go anywhere near a fibre-optic lamp, and I'd top myself before I'd let one in my house.

The woman's mouth wrinkles up as if she's sucked a lemon. 'Cheap rubbish!' she sneers. 'Waste of money!'

This, you understand, is coming from a woman who's got an artificial Christmas tree in a box tucked under her arm. I could tell her that the tree is as dodgy as the blokes she bought it from, and when she gets it home she'll probably find that the tripod stand is missing a leg, and if she tries to bring it back the stall-holders will be long gone, but I don't. I let her walk away, and I figure you're never too old to learn.

'Pigging Christmas!' Mr Fairbrother mutters. 'I'll be glad when it's over.'

'What are you going to buy your wife?' I ask, trying to make conversation.

'Don't know,' says Mr Fairbrother. 'She hasn't told me yet.'

A thousand frozen years have passed since I started this morning. Another thousand years go by, and then *I Saw Mummy Kissing Santa Claus* comes on over the speakers, which is the signal for the market to close. I box the stock, help Mr Fairbrother to dismantle the stall and pack his van. Just before he climbs into the van, Mr Fairbrother hands me the envelope that contains my wages.

'Paying you is costing me,' he says. 'I'm losing money hand over fist.'

I nearly apologise, but it isn't my fault, so I take the envelope, slip it into my pocket, say, 'See you next week,' and head for the way out.

My heart stops, because I suddenly catch sight of Adam walking towards me through the departing crowd. Adam of the bedroom eyes, the perfect jawline, the eyelashes to die for; Adam who, for some strange reason that I've never quite grasped, has been dating me for the last two months. I know exactly what it feels like to snog him, and the memory of the feeling turns my knees to mousse.

It doesn't occur to me that Adam shouldn't be here. We're supposed to meet outside the Warner Village cinema at seven o'clock. In all

5

the time we've been together, Adam's never met me from work, but I'm so pleased to see him that my alarm bells fail to ring.

Ain't love wonderful?

3

I run towards him. His eyes are drawing me. I know it's love, because when I'm with him I'm not a skinny, klutzy schoolgirl – I'm a fire-fountain, and a waterfall, and my skin is covered in stars. I can feel his name in my pulse and inside his arms is the best place I've ever been.

I'm there now. My arms are around him and I can smell him, kind of musky. I talk into his fleece. 'I wasn't expecting you!'

'I had to see you,' says Adam.

I think he means that he couldn't wait until seven, and I squeeze him tighter. I raise my head and give him a hello kiss. His lips are so cold I can hardly feel them.

He says, 'We have to talk.'

I don't like this, or the way he says it. I've seen enough soaps and movies to know that *We have to talk* isn't usually followed by good news.

'What about?' I say.

'Us.'

We walk towards the bus stop on London Road. I've got my arm through Adam's, but he's tight, tense, like he doesn't want us to touch. For a guy who has to talk, he isn't saying a lot.

'What's wrong?' I ask.

Adam sighs. 'I don't think we should go out with each other any more.' His voice is so quiet I can hardly hear him.

'Sorry?' I say.

'I don't think we should go out together any more.' His voice is louder this time. 'We're in a rut. It isn't as much fun as it used to be, is it?'

I'm – excuse me? I've been having fun, what have you been having?

'If we end it now, we can still be friends,' Adam says.

The past eight weeks zip through my head. I analyse them in detail, but I don't find any clues.

'What did I do?' I say and then, in case that isn't it, I add, 'What didn't I do?'

'Nothing. You're a great girl, Lauren. I really like you, but . . .'

'There's someone else,' I say. 'You've met someone else.' I'm convinced I'm right. When I find out who she is, I'll scratch the bitch's eyes out.

'It's us,' says Adam. 'I thought we were going somewhere at the start, but it sort of fizzled out. It's my fault. I'm not ready to be an item with anyone. I want to play the field, you know?'

8

When boys play in fields, they kick things around; this time it's me.

'We're too young to get serious,' Adam says.

He means that I care about him more than he cares about me. I thought it was the same for the both of us.

'Don't do this, Adam,' I say, and I'm shocked at how whiney I sound. 'Maybe if we talk it over, we can—'

'No. It wouldn't do any good, Lauren. I've thought about it for a long time, and I know I'm right.'

Well thanks a bunch for not mentioning anything until now!

'You'll be fine,' Adam says. 'You'll find someone else and be really happy.'

I don't want anybody but Adam. Happiness and I didn't connect until I met him. I can't go through all that again with a stranger.

I say, 'But—!'

'Let's not drag it out,' Adam says.

I want it to be some kind of test, like he's pretending to dump me to see how much I care about him, but I look in his eyes and I'm not there. He's serious. He doesn't feel anything and I'm hurting like hell. The pain's so bad that I want to wrap myself in a ball around it, and I know that it's only just started.

'See you around,' Adam says, and he walks away.

'Adam!' I shout.

He keeps right on walking.

9

Freeze-frame; zoom in to a close-up on me. This is the face of a dead girl. This is the face of a girl who's had all the light, froth and joy blasted out of her life, and all that's left is ashes.

4

On the bus ride home, I go into denial. I pile up optimistic thoughts to build a wall between me and the misery. Adam's made a mistake. After a couple of days, maybe sooner, he'll realise how much he misses me and he'll come back. What we have is too precious to throw away and too strong to be denied. This is a temporary glitch, a single sad page in a tender love story. We were meant to be together and nothing can alter that.

Behind all this stuff, fear is growing. No Adam, nothing to look forward to, nowhere to go. Life without him is impossible because he *is* my life. I can't go back to the drab little Lauren Hunter I used to be, but if Adam isn't there I can't be who I was when we were together.

Close it down; lock it away; think about Adam on my doorstep, saying, 'I was wrong, Lauren! Can we get back together, please?'

I'll say yes, because I couldn't say anything else. I'll be warm and forgiving, and everything will be all right again. I hang on to this fantasy.

If I believe in it hard enough, I can make it come true.

When I get home, the house smells of spices. Dad does the cooking at weekends and holidays, and he's whipping up one of his chilli con carnes. Again. Sarah (kid sis, fourteen, Drama Queen) is in the lounge, e-mailing her mates. I go to the kitchen. Dad's stirring a saucepan, Mum's washing rice.

Dad says, 'So there you are!'

'So here I am,' I say.

'Good day?'

'OK. Boring.'

Mum says, 'You look frozen. I'll make you a hot drink.' She abandons the rice and fills the electric kettle. 'Are you going out tonight?'

Crunch time. This is where I could tell Mum and Dad about Adam, and they'd be sympathetic and supportive. Mum would come up with a tale about some bloke who broke her heart when she was a teenager; Dad would say it's Adam's loss and that I've moved up a level in the search for Mr Right – my parents are good like that. But if I tell them, I'll start to cry, and if I cry, I'll have to admit to myself that I've got something to cry about. So I pretend that everything's fine.

'Yeah!' I say. 'I'm going to the movies with Adam. I'm meeting him in town at seven.'

Dad glances at the kitchen clock. 'I'd better get a move on,' he says.

Sarah slouches down the hall and leans in

the kitchen doorway. She has a really bad case of fourteen. Her personality changes completely every two days or so. Today she's sulky, hiding behind her long fair hair. Sarah's beautiful and boy, does she know it. It's already obvious that she's going to be far more successful with boys than I'll ever be, and it depresses me.

'You're back,' she says to me.

'No, I was abducted by aliens.'

'Oh, ha-ha! What a shame they didn't replace you with someone who has a sense of humour.' Sarah points her hair at Dad. 'What's for dinner?'

'Chilli.'

Sarah straightens herself up. 'I forgot to tell you, I'm thinking about becoming a vegetarian,' she announces.

Mum gives her a look. 'Why?'

'Because eating meat causes unnecessary suffering to animals. It's cruel to kill living things and eat them.'

'Aren't plants living things?' says Mum.

'Like peas,' says Dad in his serial-killer voice. 'We rip them off their stalks, tear them apart, boil them slowly and—'

'Stop taking the mick!' Sarah says huffily.

She's always pulling stunts like this to get attention – striking poses, taking up causes and dropping them. I can't keep up with her. Mum and Dad cope with Sarah by poking gentle fun; I ignore her. Fingers crossed, she'll grow out of being bratty soon. I'll re-establish communications then.

I eat on autopilot, even remembering to chew the food before I swallow, but I can't taste it. When I've finished, believe it or not, I toddle upstairs, shower, dress and make-up, just like I really have a date with Adam. I leave the house in time for the six-thirty bus into town, but I don't catch it. Instead, I take a walk down by the river.

The river is kind of creepy at night. In summer, homeless alcoholics hang out there, and there's plenty of undergrowth for pervs to hide in, but I'm not worried. I'm not alone. My grief is with me, and it's bigger than an American wrestler. There's no one to pretend to but myself, so I don't bother because I'm not worth it. Adam doesn't want me any more, so I'm not worth anything.

Thoughts crowd in, jostling one another to be the first in line. I'll have to come clean to my family, my friends, it'll be all round school – everyone will know. Each time I tell the story about losing Adam, I'll relive it, over and over again.

Then it gets worse. I picture Adam with someone else, doing the things that we did – laughing, kissing, touching. I know I'm torturing myself, but I can't stop.

I walk to the end of the wooden jetty opposite the university boat house, and I look at the river. The water is black and it swirls. It would be dead easy to close my eyes, step over the edge and let the current carry me away. Drowning doesn't hurt, does it? Not as badly as living does right now.

I can see what it would be like afterwards. Mum, Dad and Sarah are standing at my grave side. Adam is there too. He drops a red rose onto my coffin and weeps.

'I didn't know how much she loved me!' he wails. 'I didn't know how much I loved her, and it's too late!'

I'll be the girl no other could possibly measure up to. He'll love me forever.

I'm going to do it. I'm going to take that extra step, surrender to the dark and turn myself into a legend: Lauren Hunt, the girl who sacrificed everything for love. I take a deep breath and wait for a moment of absolute calm. I can feel destiny hurtling towards me, like a train. I lift my right foot . . .

And a voice beside me says, 'I wouldn't do that if I were you, Lauren.'

5

I jerk like I've been peeled and dipped in vinegar, and my head whips round. This guy is standing next to me. I don't know how he got there, I didn't hear a thing, and he's a complete stranger.

I say, 'Back off, buster, or I'll kick you so hard you'll be singing countertenor!'

The guy takes a step away from me, raising both hands to signal that he doesn't want any trouble.

'What are you trying to do, creeping up on me like that – give me heart failure?' I say.

He laughs. 'Considering that you were on the point of throwing yourself in the river, that really wouldn't matter, would it?' he says.

I wonder how he knows about my throwing myself in the river, but I'm too shaken to ask him. I say, 'You make a habit of hanging round here, talking to young girls?'

'No.'

'Beat it, before I call the police on my mobile.'

The guy shrugs apologetically. 'I'm afraid that I can't do that, Lauren. In your present state of mind, there's a danger that you might harm yourself.'

This makes me mad. 'What's it to you – and where do you get off calling me Lauren? Do I know you?'

'Not exactly.'

'So how come you know my name?'

The guy coughs and wriggles his shoulders. 'I take what you might term a special interest in your welfare.'

He's lit by the lamp that hangs over the boat-house doors. He's got short ginger hair and pale eyelashes. His lips are full and his nose is snubbed. His face is chubby, like the rest of him, but his features are oddly underdeveloped and he seems like an overgrown boy. He's wearing a long beige raincoat, a grey suit, white shirt and red silk tie. Put him in any office in the world and he'd fit; pass him in the street and you wouldn't look at him twice.

I think over what he's just said, and it gives me the shivers. 'Are you one of those creeps who stalk girls, find out where they live and what school they go to?'

'Certainly not!' the guy says. 'But I happen to know that your address is Six, Millbrook Close, and you attend Forest Road Comprehensive School.'

This doesn't do a whole lot for my paranoia. I whip out my mobile and switch it on.

The guy says, 'Let me assure you that I have

17

no intention of hurting you – quite the contrary.'

I punch in the first two digits. 'Yeah, yeah! Keep talking, Mr Molester.'

'Perhaps if I were to . . .' The guy scratches his forehead. 'You have a scar on your right leg,' he says. 'You fell off your tricycle when you were seven and landed on a broken bottle. Your mother took you to casualty and stayed with you while the stitches were put in. To distract you from the pain, she made up a story about a little girl who had a magic teddy bear.'

I can't dial any more because my fingers won't work. 'What?' I gasp.

'And when you were in Year Seven, you got into trouble for letting a friend copy your answers during a French vocabulary test. And at the Christmas disco in Year Eight, you refused to dance with Tim Baker, even though you were interested in him, because you didn't want him to know that you were interested.'

'You can't know that!' I say. 'I'm the only one who knows that.'

The guy purses his lips and says, 'There we are, nevertheless.'

I'm gobsmacked. I don't get this at all. One of us can't be right in the head, and I'm afraid it might be me.

'You mustn't act hastily, Lauren,' says the guy. 'You have a rich, full life ahead of you. It would be tragic to waste it because of a minor emotional setback.'

18

'What setback?'

'Adam Roden ended your relationship with him this afternoon.' The guy hesitates. 'It was this afternoon, wasn't it? That is why you're here, isn't it?'

I pull myself together. I don't know what's going on here and I don't particularly care, but I want it to end. Adopting my best, tough-cookie manner, I say, 'OK, mister. You've got ten seconds to tell me who you are, what you're doing here and how you know so much about my private life, and if I don't like your answers, you get to spend the rest of the night in a cell.'

The guy pulls at his tie, clears his throat, blushes and says, 'The name is Pontifex. I'm your guardian angel.'

6

I think, 'Huh?'

I say, 'You're *what?*'

'I'm your guardian angel,' the guy says again, with a concerned expression. 'You've heard of guardian angels, I hope? If not, I have a rather lengthy explanation to go into.'

'I know what guardian angels are,' I say. 'I just don't believe in them, that's all.'

Far from taking offence at this, the guy appears relieved. 'You don't have to,' he says. 'It's not a question of belief.'

Something strikes me here, and I immediately wish that it hadn't. I'm alone, at night, in an isolated place, with a man who might be seriously deranged. The fact that he doesn't look seriously deranged isn't particularly reassuring, since I guess that all the seriously deranged people who look seriously deranged have already been rounded up and given therapy. If I anger this guy he could turn violent, so I decide that the best thing for me to do is to humour him.

I say, 'Pontifex is an unusual name. Is it your first name or your last name?'

'It's my only name,' says Pontifex. 'It's Roman for priest.'

'You're Italian?' I say, puzzled because he doesn't sound Italian.

'No.'

'You're a Catholic?'

'No. Pontifex is an *Ancient* Roman word for a priest.'

I know it's mad, but I can't stop myself from craning my neck, trying to catch a glimpse of his back.

'What are you doing?' he asks.

He's caught me out and I'm too embarrassed to lie.

'I'm looking for your wings,' I say. 'Aren't angels meant to have wings?'

'I'm not that sort of angel.' Pontifex waves his hand as though he's brushing something aside. 'But enough of me. I'm here for you. What are you intending to do?'

He's lost me.

'Do about what?' I say.

'Your setback. Adam.'

I forgot about Adam for a moment there. Funny how talking to a person who claims to be your guardian angel can drive other thoughts out of your mind.

Pontifex gestures towards the river. 'You're not going to . . . er . . .?'

'No,' I say. 'The moment's gone. I'm not in the mood any more.'

Pontifex beams. 'I'm pleased to hear it. You

21

really should talk to someone and unburden yourself. Why don't you get in touch with—?' He breaks off and snaps his fingers in irritation. 'How stupid of me! You can't do that yet, of course. Why don't you call Jessica?'

Jessica is my best mate. Somehow it doesn't surprise me that Pontifex knows this. Nothing could surprise me tonight, because I'm obviously lost in a fantasy world. The shock of losing Adam has triggered some kind of weird psychotic reaction. Pontifex can't be my guardian angel, because he isn't actually there. Any second, I'll snap out of it and he'll disappear.

'Jessica's out on a big date,' I say.

'Ah, I was unaware of that,' says Pontifex. (So he *doesn't* know everything.) 'Isn't there another friend in whom you could confide?'

'No one as close as Jessica.' I'm not kidding. Jess and I are the way sisters ought to be.

'Your parents are generally reliable, aren't they?' Pontifex says tactfully.

'Pretty much.'

'Why not confide in them then?'

'Good idea,' I say.

And it *is* a good idea. Things have been as bad as they can get. I've teetered on the brink of ending it all and stepped back, and talking to Mum and Dad doesn't seem so bad as it did earlier.

The atmosphere turns awkward. I get the impression that Pontifex has done what he came to do, our conversation is at an end and I should leave, but I don't know how. What's the drill for leaving an angel?

'Well, I'd better be going,' I say. God, it sounds lame!

Pontifex is as much at a loss as I am. 'Should I accompany you?' he offers.

In my imagination, I hear myself saying, '*Hi, Mum! Hi, Dad! This is Pontifex, my guardian angel.*'

'No!' I yelp. 'I'll be fine.' This seems a little ungrateful, so I add, 'Thanks for your help.'

Pontifex gives me a slight bow. 'You're entirely welcome.'

I start to walk away, and something is niggling at me. I stop, turn and say, 'Pontifex, are you for real or is this a dream?'

Pontifex thinks, then says, 'It's probably better not to know.'

I think he's probably right.

On the way home, I notice that I've changed. The same problems are facing me, but my attitude is different. My hurt about Adam is just about bearable, and after I've survived it, I'll have a new life. I have no idea what it'll be like, and that's exciting. Adam's a mistake I won't make again. People who die for the sake of love have to be desperate, or dumb (or both), because the whole point of being in love is to stay alive so that you can enjoy it. This simple truth has never occurred to me before.

23

I could almost laugh at myself for getting suicidal. Almost, but not quite.

At home, I have a lucky break – the Brat has gone to a friend's house, and I have my parents to myself.

'You're back early,' Mum says.

I pour out my heart, together with a few tears which are only self-pity leaking through my eyes. I wind up on the sofa, in the middle of a three-way cuddle.

'Adam is a jerk,' says Dad. 'There are a lot better boys than him around.'

Mum says, 'You know, when I was your age, I had a terrible crush on a boy called Geoff . . .'

Parents: they drive you nuts with their nagging and interfering, but there are times when no one else will do, aren't there?

7

Next morning there's this gap inside me where Adam used to be, and it hurts like a missing milk-tooth. I hang on until gone eleven, then I phone Jess on my mobile.

'Hi,' I say. 'Adam broke up with me yesterday.'

The line goes dead.

Twenty minutes later, Jess is ringing the front-door bell.

Jess is the best friend in the entire history of the universe and I love her to bits, but she doesn't do a lot to improve my self-esteem. She has green eyes, glossy auburn hair and cheekbones like the blade of a plough. Her legs won't quit and she has a figure that makes jets of steam come out of guys' ears. When we go out together, I don't get a look in, and if a couple of boys chat us up, guess who gets the dork? But I'll forgive Jess anything. We've been mates since our first day at Forest Road Comp. We took one look at each other, burst out laughing for no apparent reason and we've been laughing ever since – and crying, and standing up for each other, and all that stuff that mates do.

As soon as we're up in my bedroom, Jess says, 'Is Adam serious?'

'He didn't smile a whole lot,' I say.

'What happened?'

I tell her. I don't cry, but it's a close call.

'The rat!' says Jess. 'That's what he did to Jenny Fisher.'

'And Bindi Johnson,' I remind her.

'You know Adam's problem?' says Jess. 'He's terrified of commitment. He can't handle the responsibility. When a relationship threatens to go serious on him, he's out of there. He's an emotional coward.'

'Tight buns though.'

'You can't build a future on tight buns,' says Jess, which puts all kinds of weird pictures in my head. 'What did you do last night?'

I know that some day I'll be able to tell Jess about Pontifex, but not today. First I have to figure him out for myself.

'I went for a stroll,' I say vaguely. 'I considered throwing myself in the river, but I didn't.'

'Good!' says Jess. 'After all, Adam's just a bloke. It isn't the end of the world.'

'I know. I've filed him under *Older but Wiser*. How was your date?'

It was going to be Jess's Big Moment. She and Sam Collard have had a thing for each other for ages, but Sam was an item with

26

Danielle James. Danielle gave Sam the boot a week ago, and Jess was straight in there with her sympathetic shoulder and drop-dead looks.

Jess rolls her eyes and wrinkles her nose. 'Sam is such a loser!' she says. 'He spent the whole night comparing me with Danielle. He didn't say anything about her, but I could tell what he was thinking. Plus he's a lousy snogger – two out of ten.'

Two out of ten means a slobberer.

'Did he ask you for another date?' I say.

'I managed to avoid it.'

'How?'

'I told him not to ask me out again,' says Jess, 'and I told him he should remember to swallow before he kisses anyone.'

Jess, as you will have gathered, is not big in the punch-pulling department.

'So, what now?' I say.

'Now I'm like you,' says Jess. 'Young, hot and unattached. What say we go clubbing on Wednesday night to celebrate the end of term?'

I shrug. 'I'm not sure I feel like clubbing.'

'Sure you're sure!' says Jess. 'This Christmas, we're going to party till we drop. Who knows, we could meet the men of our dreams.'

'I'm still working on my dreams,' I say.

As always, talking to Jess makes me feel better, and she leaves me on a high.

I do the family Sunday-lunch thing. This week it's roast lamb with mint sauce. Sarah's

27

evidently forgotten about vegetarianism and chugs down three helpings. Where does she put it?

I'm quiet. I have a lot on my mind. Mum and Dad assume that I'm moping over Adam, but it isn't that. Sarah doesn't notice. If I had a spear sticking through me, Sarah would say, 'What's up, misery guts?'

What's on my mind is Pontifex. He sort of saved my life last night, and it's left me with a load of questions that I can't answer. Even if he was a figment of my imagination, he was there right when I needed him, which makes him a kind of miracle, doesn't it? I feel that I owe someone a big thank you, and I have a sneaking suspicion that I know who that somebody is.

I stand up and say, 'I'm going out for a while.'

Mum looks anxious. 'You're not going to see Adam, are you?' she says.

'No,' I say. 'I'm going to church.'

The silence is amazing. Everybody freezes: Sarah's fork is stopped in mid air; Dad's mouth is hanging open; Mum's eyes are bulging.

It must be the way I tell 'em.

8

In terms of Big Questions, God is right up there with the meaning of life and why the cling-film wrappers on video cassettes are such a hassle to remove. I don't think about God often, because it reminds me of the RE teacher I had in Year Eight, who was enough to put anyone off religion. Mum and Dad are atheists, but they've always left me alone to believe what I like. I did go to Sunday school once with this girl I was friends with in the Juniors, but it was boring and left me with no desire to repeat the experience. To me, God is *Songs of Praise*, morning assembly and weird people who knock on the door and ask if I've accepted Jesus as my personal saviour – like it was any business of theirs. I've got myself pegged as an agnostic and figure that if God wants me to believe in him, he'll send me a sign. Which he might just have done, in the shape of Pontifex. If Pontifex *is* a sign, there must be more to this God stuff than I realised, so maybe I should investigate. I'm open-minded about most things, barring party-political broadcasts and line-dancing. I won't get any answers at home, so I reckon a church is the way to go. I'm thinking – sympathetic vicar, bit of a chat, see the light, back in time for tea.

I climb the hill and turn right onto Church Road. I can see the spire of St Peter's sticking up above the rooftops. St Peter's is one of those Victorian Gothic jobs with knobbly bits and gargoyles. It happens to be an Anglican church, but that has nothing to do with it. The reason I've chosen St Peter's is that it has a row of cherry trees outside, and in spring the blossom is the colour of strawberry ice cream, so the church seems kind of festive. If you want logic, go talk to a physicist.

I pause at the lych-gate (yes, I had to look up what it's called) and stare at the building. There's not a strawberry ice cream in sight, and suddenly St Peter's doesn't look festive, in fact it's positively forbidding. A chill wind blows across the churchyard and moans in the roof of the lych-gate, and we are talking creepy. The gate shrieks when I open it and shuts with a clunk that sounds ominously final. I regret all the hours I spent watching old horror movies on late-night TV.

One thing keeps me going: there must have been a wedding here recently, because there's confetti at the side of the path, and I tune in to the echoes of the happy event. People with more complicated questions than mine must have come to St Peter's over the years. I just want to know why I met my guardian angel – nothing fancy.

In the porch of the church, I encounter the teensiest problemette. The door is closed. And padlocked. And fitted with an alarm and a CCTV security camera. Is the congregation afraid that somebody will break in and steal their faith?

Behind me, a voice says, 'Looking for someone?'

I recognise the voice as Pontifex's. There goes my secret hope that he was a one-off delusion. I turn slowly and say, 'Yeah. God, actually.'

Pontifex looks puzzled. 'And you came here?'

'Where else?'

'Anywhere else,' says Pontifex. 'This place is of no use to you – it's shut.'

I begin to think I may have made a stupid mistake. 'I just wanted to pop in and say a quick thank you,' I say.

'A prayer?'

'Something like that.'

Pontifex looks even more puzzled. 'But you don't say prayers. You're not the praying kind.'

'Not usually,' I agree. 'But I thought meeting you last night counted as a special occasion.'

Pontifex isn't pleased. 'Lauren, you seem to have misunderstood,' he says. 'I'm not here to convert you.'

'So why are you here?'

'Because it's where you are.'

I twig that this is one of those conversations that goes round and round, and I try to break the loop.

'What's he like?' I say.

'Who?'

'God.'

Pontifex grins, like he was expecting me to ask. 'You don't seriously expect me to answer that question, do you?' he says.

'Can't you drop a few hints?'

Pontifex shakes his head. 'It's a private matter. You have to find your own way.'

'I have been,' I say. 'It hasn't really involved God so far.'

'Then why involve him now?'

It strikes me that when it comes to PR work, Pontifex sucks. I laugh and say, 'You're not much of an angel, are you?'

'I'm as much of an angel as I can be,' Pontifex says.

He sounds so sincere that the laughter dies in my throat. I shiver; Pontifex notices.

'You're cold,' he says. 'Shall we walk? The exercise will be good for your circulation.'

We wander around the churchyard. This is the first time I've seen Pontifex in daylight. He's even less impressive than he was last night. His raincoat is creased, his shoes are muddy, his tie is pulled to one side and there's a faint grey ring around the edge of his shirt-collar.

I say, 'Where did you spend the night – in a ditch?'

It's meant as a joke, but the glance that Pontifex gives me tells me that it's too true to be funny.

'On a park bench,' he says.

'Don't you get travelling expenses and an accommodation allowance?'

'The arrangements for my accommodation are neither here nor there,' Pontifex says. 'We have more urgent matters to consider.'

'Such as?'

'The future. Your friend Jessica's advice is worth taking. You should go out and enjoy yourself, but be careful. When you go to the club on Wednesday, you will—'

'Hold it right there!' I growl. 'Do you know what's going to happen to me?'

'To a limited extent.'

'Do me a favour and keep it to yourself, Pontifex. I don't want to know.'

I mean it; I've never wanted to know. The thought that Destiny has planned our lives and we act them out like puppets is pretty disturbing, if you ask me.

Pontifex says, 'But—'

'No!'

'I'm simply attempting to—'

'Don't,' I say. 'I like surprises.'

'As you wish,' says Pontifex. 'Your stubborn attitude makes my task more difficult, but it can't be helped.'

33

I try to slip in a sly one under his guard. 'And what is your task, exactly?'

No dice. Pontifex is silent – smugly, maddeningly silent.

'Is that another question I shouldn't seriously expect you to answer?' I say.

'I thought you preferred to do things the hard way,' says Pontifex.

You'd think that, if he is a product of my imagination, I'd have come up with a guardian angel who was less of a smart-ass, wouldn't you?

'I must go,' I say.

It's true. The cold has got to my bladder.

'I know,' says Pontifex. 'Take care. We'll be in touch.'

I leave him at the lych-gate. After a few metres, I turn to give Pontifex a wave, but he's nowhere in sight. Either he can move incredibly fast for a chubby guy, or he's hiding. I don't dwell on this for long because I have more pressing concerns – like getting to a loo as soon as possible.

9

School and Monday morning – deadly combination. Don't be in such a rush to grow up, remember that you have to go through school to get there. At the moment, school is a major pain because it's the fag-end of term. The pantomime has finished, the carol concert has been and gone. We had our mock GCSE results last week. (I think they're called *mocks* because the teachers say, 'Hah!' when they give you back your answer papers.) My results were OK, not as bad as I'd feared, not as good as I'd hoped. Now all the traumas are over, the staff are killing time, child-minding until the holidays start. So it's word searches, work sheets and stuff the teachers regard as fun activities. If you've been there, you'll understand; if you haven't, you don't want to know.

We have a discussion in Social Ed – surprise, surprise! *Does Christmas have any spiritual significance in the modern age?* Er, didn't we cover that this time last year? And anyway, where's the discussion? If you're a spiritual person *everything* has a spiritual significance, and if you're not, nothing does.

My attention meanders around the classroom. Angels are everywhere – on the Christmas cards stuck around the whiteboard, dangling from the ceiling, on bits of string. I can't get away from them, so I don't try. English is a free-reading session in the school library, and I take the opportunity to hit the angel-books.

Let me tell you up front, some of what's been written about angels is *right* out there! They're God's messengers, and in Chapter Ten of Mark's gospel, Jesus says that they protect children. A helpful encyclopaedia informs me that angels aren't exclusively Judaeo-Christian. The Hittites and the Canaanites had them too – whoever they were. At the end of my research, I know less than when I started and I'm none the wiser about Pontifex or what his task is.

I eat lunch with Jess in the cafeteria, then we mosey over to the Year Eleven Recreational Area, which is just a room with a table-football table and a cheap stereo – but hey, it's home. I'm nervous about going there, because there's a distinct possibility that I'll run into Adam, and I'm not sure how I'll react. Weeping in the Recreational Area is definitely uncool. But it turns out that I've worried for nothing; it's an Adam-free zone. Almost, that is. His ghost is still there. The grapevine's been putting in some overtime: I keep getting sympathetic

36

glances, plus knowing smirks and people whispering behind their hands as they stare at me.

I'm not the only girl who's been messed around by Adam. I wonder if we should form a club, and then it seems we might, because Jenny Fisher comes over, plonks herself in the chair next to mine and says, 'I hear Adam Roden dumped you.'

'You hear right,' I say.

'That's what he did to me.'

'I know. Not nice, is it?'

'I think you're very brave,' Jenny says. 'After he finished with me, I couldn't stop crying for a week.'

She seems proud of this; I can't imagine why.

'I guess it affects different people in different ways,' I say.

'It all works out for the best in the end,' says Jenny. 'I was just a girl before I went out with Adam. Now I'm with David. He's far more mature.'

She means Dave Jessop, who is possibly the biggest love-rat who ever walked. Dave is all hormones, has the attention span of a gnat and Jenny is the only person in the world who would ever think of him as mature.

Jess sniggers and converts it into a cough; she'll have me going in a minute.

'I wanted to let you know that I understand,' says Jenny. 'There is life after Adam, you know – look at me!'

I don't know how I do this, but I keep a

straight face and say, 'Thanks, Jenny. I appreciate it.'

Having spread a little sunshine, Jenny flits off.

Jess's face is red with suppressed laughter. 'There you are!' she gurgles. 'Look on the bright side. Some day, you could be another Jenny and date someone like Dave Jessop.'

'Don't make me go there!' I moan.

'You up for Wednesday night?' Jess says, in full won't-take-no-for-an-answer mode.

'Yeah,' I say. 'Ponti – er, a friend told me it would be good for me.'

Fatal slip; Jess thinks that someone's muscling in on her patch.

'Oh?' she says. 'What friend was that?'

I improvise; it comes out as gabble. 'Not a *friend* friend, more of a family acquaintance.'

'Which family acquaintance?' Jess says; she's not going to let this one go.

'My Mum's second cousin, or something. He dropped by after lunch yesterday. He saw I was down, asked me about it and I told him.'

Frostiness from Jess.

'I didn't go into details,' I add. 'Not like when I told you.'

Jess defrosts slightly, and I've got away with it.

Help, I'm lying to my best mate! Meeting Pontifex has made me more deceitful and devious.

38

Are guardian angels supposed to have that effect on you?

10

Now we cut to one of those corny montages that show the passage of time: pages peeling off calendars; speeded-up clocks with whizzing hands. This is my way of showing that nothing much happens the rest of Monday and all day Tuesday. I go home, eat, sleep, wake up and go to school. I have no profound thoughts or startling insights, no visitations from Pontifex, no phone-calls from Adam pleading to get back together – zilch.

I go up and down like a fairground ride. Up is feeling good about myself: Christmas is party season and parties are full of possibilities. Down is when I miss Adam: he made me special; a word or a look from him could make or break my day; without him, I'm a vacuum.

Also there's Pontifex. I try to put him on hold, but he keeps weaselling his way out. I reckon that my subconscious mind cooked him up and that he's only there for me – like in those movies where the main character talks to a ghost that no one else can see? I don't *think* that I'm cracking up, but it's hard to tell. Can you tell when you're cracking up, or does everything seem normal – or, in my case, abnormal?

I wish I could talk to someone about this, but it would sound too crazy. I mean, if someone else told me about me, I wouldn't believe them. It doesn't seem to be doing me any harm though, apart from the devious thing, that is. I'm not developing a morbid interest in firearms or embroidery; I don't feel the urge to pick up an orange crayon and a sheet of brown paper, and write a rambling letter to the Prime Minister. Maybe I need Pontifex to help me get over Adam. If I'm patient and keep my cool, Pontifex will go away and I'll be OK again.

I hope.

11

Term ends on Wednesday afternoon. After lunch, Jess and I return to our form base for a final registration. We help to stack chairs on tables, and then there's an irritating thirty-minute wait, with nothing to do and nowhere to sit while we do it.

Jess says, 'What are you planning on wearing tonight?'

'A sack,' I say.

'How about your silver number?'

'That silver dress was a mistake,' I say. 'It makes me look like I've been wrapped in baking foil. What are you going to wear?'

'Oh, I'll find something,' Jess says airily.

She will, and it'll take her about two hours. Appearance is important to Jess which, given her looks, is understandable, but sometimes I think that she sells herself short. There's more to her than beauty and a terrific figure. She's intelligent, funny, sensitive and don't you just hate people who have it all?

The bell rings. We pile out of the room, into the gridlocked corridor. Some people are wearing furry antler-things on their heads, others are wrapped in tinsel boas; boys with loser-faces are waving sprigs of mistletoe.

'Can I tell you something?' says Jess.

She means can she tell me something about myself that would be offensive if it came from anyone else.

'Go ahead,' I say, gritting my teeth.

'I'm glad that it's over between you and Adam.'

'You are?'

'Yes,' says Jess. 'He wasn't good for you, Lauren. The past few weeks you've been . . .' Jess frowns. 'Not you, you know?'

'So who have I been?'

'Adam's girlfriend. It was like he'd taken you over, and you were disappearing.'

'You didn't say anything,' I point out.

'You told me you were happy. I didn't want to spoil it,' Jess says. 'Anyway, it's against the rules to come between a mate and her man. If I'd said, you would've thought I was jealous.'

'And were you?'

'Not jealous of you, but I was a bit jealous of Adam. He took up so much of you, there was no room left for me. You shouldn't have to drop your friends because of some bloke.'

Jess is onto something. Adam, it begins to dawn on me, likes being adored, and when you're in a relationship with him, thou shalt not have any other gods. He picked which movies we went to, the places we'd meet; he

43

called the shots and expected me to drop every-thing to suit him. And I did.

'You're right!' I say. 'OK, I swear – no more domineering males. No more all-take-and-no-give guys.'

Jess high-fives me. 'Way to go, girlfriend!'

I have an up that lasts until I get home.

Sarah is already in, watching TV. We both go to Forest Road Comp, but we don't go there together. I paid my dues when Sarah was in the Infants, and I had to walk home with her every day. Her friends called me 'Sarah's sister'. It's always been that way round; Sarah's never been called, 'Lauren's sister'.

Sarah gives me an indignant look – narrowed eyes, bottom lip stuck out. 'You didn't tell me about Adam!' she says.

'I didn't think you'd be interested,' I say.

'Do Mum and Dad know?'

'I told them on Saturday night.'

Sarah folds her arms under her budding bosom. 'No one tells me anything in this family!' she grumbles. 'I had to find out from Stephanie King. I felt like a right plonker.'

Sarah loathes being behind with the goss.

'Mum and Dad and I weren't ganging up on you behind your back,' I say.

'Huh!' says Sarah, then she relents a bit. 'Did you chuck him or did he chuck you?'

'He chucked me.'

'I'd never let a boy do that to me. If I thought he was going to chuck me, I'd get in first.'

44

'It's not that simple,' I say.

'Didn't you see it coming?'

I say, 'No,' but thinking back, that's not strictly accurate. There was that evening when I went over to Adam's, and found him playing some stupid Nintendo game with his mates. Adam hardly said a word to me. I put up with it, because being in his company was enough.

'You won't catch me letting a boy use me as a doormat!' says Sarah.

'You'll go far, sis,' I say. I gaze at her and think, 'Is this it? Is this the breakthrough that's going to change us from squabbling siblings to good buddies?'

Sarah says, 'How could you be so dumb?'

That answers that question then.

12

I meet Jess in town and we join the modest mid-week queue outside Aardvarks. Aardvarks isn't the UK's trendiest or most exciting club, but it's the only show in town and the music's not bad. The bouncers at the door give us the once-over and let us in. We check in our coats at the cloakroom. Jess's outfit makes her look like a princess and I feel dowdy standing next to her, until we hit the dance floor.

The seismic pulse of the beat throbs through me. I give in to it, let it take me where it wants me to go, and all at once I'm not in Aardvarks. I'm flying above the surface of a huge dark ocean; I'm bursting out of the cone of a volcano; I'm riding a comet to another galaxy. I wave my arms – bye-bye, school! I shake my head – bye-bye, Adam! The rhythm of the music transforms my problems into movement, and I dance them away. I know the relief will only be temporary, but as temporary reliefs go, it's among the best.

Boys come and go, cruising in pairs. I don't really notice them; it's the dance in me, dancing with the dance in them. My partners are either stiff and self-conscious, or totally wild; there's no connection between us.

After an hour, dancing is getting to be hard work, so Jess and I take a breather. We go to the bar area and I fork out an extortionate amount of money for two plastic beakers of Diet Coke. Every table is occupied, so we find an empty bit of wall to lean against.

Jess says, 'Two guys over there are looking at us.'

'Looking at you, you mean,' I say.

'No. One of them only has eyes for you.'

'Don't tell me!' I say. 'He's puny, spotty and dressed in black, right?'

'Actually, they're both quite tasty.'

Now I'm interested. 'Which guys?'

'Third table on the right from the men's loos.'

In a way that I hope is cool and casual, I look. Then it's not so casual, because I lock eyes with the guy that Jess told me about. Hunk alert! He's got close-cropped blond hair, a slightly-crooked nose that's kind of cute and shoulders like he works out. He smiles at me.

I say, 'Oh, my God, he's smiling at me!'

'Smile back!' says Jess.

Smiling to order isn't easy, as you'll know from the photographs you've seen of yourself trying to do it. I give it a bash and the effect is instant. The guy stands up.

I say, 'Oh, my God, he's standing up!'

'Take it easy!' Jess hisses.

47

The guy approaches us and says, 'Excuse me, but my friend and I couldn't help noticing that you have nowhere to sit. Would you care to join us?'

The line is as smoothly-worn as a pebble on the bed of a stream, but his delivery is charming.

'Sure!' says Jess. 'Why not?'

We go over to the table.

The guy says, 'I'm Craig and this is Josh.'

'Jessica,' says Jess.

'Lauren,' I say.

'Lauren is a lovely name,' says Craig.

'Thanks.'

'Aren't you going to tell me that my name's lovely?'

Well, what d'you know! Craig has a sense of humour and a brain.

Jess and I sit down. Jess and Josh start rabbiting away.

'What do you do, Lauren?' Craig asks.

'I'm still at school,' I say.

'In the Sixth Form?'

A strategic lie is called for here, because Craig is at least nineteen.

'Hmm,' I say.

'What are you studying?'

'English, History and French. What d'you do?'

'I'm training to be a chartered surveyor.'

I don't know what this means, and I'm about to sink without trace, when the DJ throws me

48

a lifeline. He puts on last summer's big club hit, the one that nobody can resist. There's a general rush for the floor, that includes Jess and Josh.

'Would you care to dance?' says Craig.

I'd care to; it's safer than conversation.

Craig is good; Craig is *very* good. He shadows my moves, adds subtle variations, anticipates when I'm going to change direction. It's synchronised swimming with no water; we've connected.

The track is a remix that goes on and on. When it finally fades out, the DJ plays something slow so that people can chill.

Craig dances closer, rests his hands on my shoulders. He leans forward and whispers, 'Why don't you—?'

The rest of the question is yukky. The rest of the question pushes me away from him and off the floor, heading for the lobby. I'm close to tears. I came out tonight looking for something that would help me to patch up my self-respect, and I got hit on by a sleaze who takes me for a tart. I don't need this and I have to escape from it.

Just to make my joy complete, I collide with a guy and his drink sloshes all over me.

'I'm so sorry!' he says. 'Can I get you a tissue to—?'

I'm humiliated, dripping and in no mood for politeness.

'You can get out of my face!' I screech.

49

In the lobby, I give my ticket to the cloak-room attendant, put on my coat over my wet things and leave.

Just as I step onto the street, Jess comes running after me.

'Lauren, are you all right?' she says.

'No.'

'What's the matter?'

I tell her what Craig asked me to do.

'Eew, gross!' says Jess.

'I'm going home,' I say. 'I need a shower and a packet of chocolate biscuits.'

'Wait for me. I'll get my coat and come with you.'

'I don't want to ruin your fun, Jess.'

'It's already ruined,' Jess says.

She's such a brilliant mate. She wouldn't be on her own if she stayed, because there are plenty of girls from school in the club and she could easily pal up with any of them, but Jess chooses to keep me company instead.

'I'm sorry, Lauren,' she says. 'It was my idea.'

'It was your idea, but it wasn't your fault,' I say. 'Why do I never get the good guys, Jess?'

Jess doesn't attempt an answer, because there isn't one.

'Shall we grab a coffee somewhere?' she says.

'No. I'm working at the market tomorrow. I might as well get an early night.' (I'm working at the market all day tomorrow and on Friday,

50

which is Christmas Eve. Great start to the holiday, isn't it?)

Jess says, 'Don't let one scumbag spoil things for you. The good guy is around somewhere. He's probably wondering where you are.'

'Yeah?' I say. 'Well I wish he'd put more effort into finding me.'

Jess and I catch different buses. Mine is a double decker. I go upstairs and it's completely empty, which suits me fine because I need room for my misery. I sit in the front seat, like I did when I was a kid.

I'm really down. Is this how it's going to be, years of slime-balls, control freaks and ego-maniacs? It must be me. I must have this major flaw in my personality that attracts the wrong kind of person. I might as well give up. If I could switch straight from adolescence to frumpy middle-age, I'd do it.

Someone clumps up the stairs, lumbers down the aisle and sits down next to me.

It's Pontifex.

13

'I tried to warn you, but would you listen? No!' says Pontifex. 'Headstrong, that's what you are. Now you're feeling sorry for yourself, aren't you?'

'No, I'm wallowing in self-pity,' I say.

'You only have yourself to blame for that. You fixed your attention on the wrong incident, and this is the result.'

'Which incident should I have fixed my attention on?'

'Shan't tell you!' Pontifex says sulkily.

His suit is creased, as well as his raincoat. The top button is missing from his shirt, his collar is downright grubby and there are stains on his tie. He's having trouble focussing and his voice is thick. I catch a sniff of his breath and it makes my eyes water.

'Pontifex, have you been drinking?' I say.

Pontifex blinks in a dignified manner. 'I may have shared a bottle with an obliging vagrant, but not in sufficient quantity to impair my ability to protect your best interests.'

I'm honestly surprised. 'I didn't know angels could get drunk,' I say.

'Your ignorance about angels could fill volumes.'

'There's no need to be personal.'

'A guardian angel has no choice other than to be personal,' Pontifex says.

His flippancy annoys me, so I get personal too. 'Speaking of which,' I say, 'you've been doing a pretty sloppy job so far, haven't you?'

'I beg your pardon?'

'You didn't stop Adam from finishing with me, you didn't stop that guy in Aardvarks from coming on to me – in fact, where were you in my life when all the rubbish stuff happened?'

'My function isn't to prevent, but to temper,' Pontifex says grandly. 'Your experiences could have been far worse, you know.'

I notice that, according to the reflection in the bus window, the seat next to me is empty.

'You don't have a reflection,' I say.

'True,' says Pontifex. 'Glass is too coarse a medium to capture my ethereal essence.'

'Are you always like this when you're drunk?'

'Like what?'

'Wordy?'

'I don't know,' says Pontifex. 'This is my first time. Now, about Friday—'

I don't want to hear it. 'When are you going to make a difference?' I demand. 'When are you going to do something for me?'

'When you do something for yourself,' Pontifex says.

This is a cracking comeback and I wish I

had time to discuss it, but it's my stop next. I ring the bell.

'I'm getting off,' I say. 'Are you coming?'

Pontifex hiccups. 'I think not,' he says. 'I'm feeling rather tired. Good night, dear child! May flights of angels sing thee to thy rest.'

I go downstairs, muttering to myself. Take it from me, there's no point in trying to get sense out of your guardian angel after he's had a few.

14

The alarm wakes me at quarter to six – as in, 05:45. I shut it off and roll out of bed, running on sheer willpower. Some people have to get up at this time every morning to earn a living and I hope I don't turn out to be one of them. I go to the bathroom, perform my ablutions (love that expression!), get dressed in my market gear and stumble downstairs. I'm not conscious yet, I'm still asleep, having this awful dream about having to get ready for work.

Dad has gatecrashed my dream. He's in the kitchen, boiling eggs and dropping slices of bread into the toaster, wearing a striped apron over his office suit.

'What's this?' I say.

'This is me, cooking your breakfast before I give you a lift,' says Dad. 'Take a pew.'

I sit at the breakfast bar. 'But you don't have to be at the office until nine,' I say.

'They won't fire me for being early.'

'But—!'

Dad waves a slotted spoon at me. 'Lauren, if I decide that my daughter could use a little

TLC, it's my affair, OK? You want your toast cut into soldiers?'

This touches one of the warmest places I know. After Sarah was born, it felt like I'd been knocked off the Number One spot. I used to sneak down early so that I could share Dad's breakfast and have him to myself.

'Yes, please,' I say. 'Dad, can I ask you something?'

'As long as it isn't complicated.'

'More than half the kids in my form have divorced parents, but you and Mum are still together.'

Dad puts two boiled eggs and a plate of soldiers in front of me. 'And?' he says.

'What's the secret?'

'No secret. You meet the right person and you don't let go.'

'That's all?'

'Almost. First you have to find the right person. That's the difficult part.'

'How d'you know that they're the right person?'

'Faith.'

'Faith in what?'

'Eat your eggs before they get cold,' Dad says.

He's copping out, but I don't push him, because I figure he's already doing enough for me.

Eating rouses my brain, and I try to work out the difference between belief and faith. I always thought that they were the same, but they're not. Your beliefs can alter, and they evolve as you learn more. Faith is stuff you just know deep down inside, like Dad knows that he loves Mum, and he can't be argued out of it. I'll be that way about somebody one day. With Adam, it wasn't love so much as gratitude – I was knocked out that he even noticed me. What Jess said about me not being myself was bang on. I'm not even sure that I like the person I was then – she was a wimp.

Dad and I finish breakfast, clear away and go out to the car. It's dark, but a grey dawn is breaking. I can't remember the last time I saw a blue sky. I like winter when it's bright and crisp, but today it's cold and dreary, and too much like I feel.

Dad drives through the estate and takes a right onto London Road. I don't know where his mind has been, but right out of nowhere he says, 'Making mistakes is part of the process.'

'Excuse me?' I say.

'Relationships,' says Dad. 'As the saying goes, you have to kiss a lot of frogs before one of them turns into a prince.'

I store this in a safe place for future reference.

Dad drops me off at the airfield. I'm early, so I hang around the parking area, waiting for Mr Fairbrother. He arrives at ten to seven and, wait for it, *he's in a good mood!* He smiles at me and says, 'Good morning, Laura.'

57

He's been calling me Laura for months. I haven't had the nerve to correct him.

Mr Fairbrother rubs his hands. 'Only gone and cracked it, haven't I?' he says.

'You have?'

Mr Fairbrother chortles. 'Came to me last night.' He mimes a bolt of lightning striking his head. 'Should've thought of it before.'

'Thought of what?'

'The hard sell,' says Mr Fairbrother. 'It's no use standing about waiting for customers. You have to grab their attention and make them come to you. Wait till you see this!'

Mr Fairbrother opens the back door of the van, takes out a large sheet of card and holds it up. Written on the card in black felt-tip pen is: *GET YOUR FIBER OPTIC LAMPS HERE.*

'Well?' says Mr Fairbrother. 'What d'you think?'

I say, 'Shouldn't fibre be R-E, not E-R?'

'American spelling,' Mr Fairbrother says. 'Punters go for American stuff – it's contemporary. I'll be quids in by the end of the day, you mark my words!'

Despite the attention-grabbing, hard-sell sign, between eight and twelve thirty, we only sell one lamp, but then business is slow everywhere. Most of the punters are elderly and not into fibre-optics.

Mr Fairbrother's faith remains undented. 'Trade will pick up later,' he says. 'You go for your lunch, Laura. I'll hold the fort.'

I stroll over to Joe's Diner, a converted ice-cream van that serves fast food. Joe does wicked bacon rolls. They're packed with cholesterol – a heart seizure in every bite – but you don't count the calories when it's perishing cold, and it's like eating a warm duvet. I swill down the last of the grease with a mug of brick-red tea, and I'm fit for anything.

And then, on my way back to the stall, something in the air goes – POP! – and the mood of the market changes. It's bustling and excited. I can't put my finger on the change, and I don't get the chance to think about it, because the stall is surrounded by people going, 'Ooh!' and 'Ahh!' They're staring at the merchandise and they seem to be in a trance.

Mr Fairbrother is giving it loads. 'Step right up, folks!' he bawls. 'Fibre-optic lamps, hand-built by Taiwanese master craftsmen. They're modern! They're mysterious! They're seven pounds fifty!'

Everybody wants one. I box and bag my buns off. It's never been like this before, and it doesn't let up.

Time passes too quickly for me to be bored.

By four o'clock we're down to our last three lamps, and there's a welcome lull.

'I think I'll call it a day,' says Mr Fairbrother. 'Let's get shifting, Laura.'

I chance my arm and say, 'Lauren.'

'You what?'

'My name is Lauren.'

59

'Oh, aye?' says Mr Fairbrother. 'Like Lauren Bacall, eh?'

'Like who?'

'Never mind,' says Mr Fairbrother. 'You might learn about her in History.'

'We pack up. Mr Fairbrother gives me my wages, then hands me a twenty-pound note. 'Bonus,' he says. 'You've earned it.'

I'm dazed. I don't know what Mrs Fairbrother slipped into her husband's tea this morning, but I want some too.

Mr Fairbrother says, 'I expect you'll be glad of an early finish. You'll be able to see more of your young man.'

'I don't have a young man at the moment,' I say.

Mr Fairbrother gasps. 'No young man? What's wrong with the boys round here – are they blind?'

It isn't until after he's driven off that I realise Mr Fairbrother was paying me a compliment.

Seeing as I've got an extra twenty quid and time to play with, I go hunting for Sarah's Christmas present. I've got Mum a bottle of perfume, and Dad a nodding dog for the back of his car (yeah, I know, but he likes nodding dogs). I was going to give Sarah a record token, but it might be more thoughtful to buy her an actual record.

I find the perfect gift on the CD stall – the latest release from Ladzcape, complete with promotional poster. Sarah's keen on Ladzcape, and shudders with lust every time she sees them on TV. I don't know if she likes their music, but she can always drool over the poster.

'It's for my sister,' I tell the stall-holder.

'That right?' he says, like it's more information than he needs.

I don't want anyone to get the idea that I'm a fan of Ladzcape – I'm too old for that kind of thing!

I turn to leave, and find myself face to face with Pontifex. He looks rough. There are bags under his eyes and his skin is the colour of vanilla yoghurt.

'Can't you let me know in advance when you're going to turn up?' I say. 'Like give me a call or something?'

'No telephone,' Pontifex says. He has a shifty look in his eyes, as if he's been up to no good.

In my mind, I hear the heavy clunking of things falling into place.

'It was you!' I say.

'It still is me,' says Pontifex.

'You made all those customers visit the stall, didn't you?'

'I thought you wanted me to make a difference.'

'I do, but not by turning people into consumer-zombies!'

Pontifex looks at his fingernails, which are filthy. 'There's no pleasing some people,' he says. 'Last night you chided me for doing

61

nothing, now you're chiding me for encouraging business.'

'You can't do this, Pontifex!' I snap. 'It's wrong to interfere with people like that!'

'There's a fine balance between right and wrong, but I hardly think that the purchase of a few lamps will throw the universe into chaos,' Pontifex says.

I don't want to argue with him; he looks too fragile.

'Hangover?' I say.

Pontifex nods. 'It's nothing – just agony.'

'Serves you right!'

'I hear that if I swallow a dog's hair, the pain will go away.'

It takes me a sec to get my head around this. 'No, Pontifex,' I explain, 'a hair of the dog means that you should have another drink. It's an old saying.'

'So many colloquialisms, so little time!' Pontifex says with a sigh. 'We really must talk about Friday.'

'No we mustn't,' I say. I take a fiver from what's left of my bonus and thrust it into Pontifex's hand. 'There's a pub about two kilometres up the road. Have one on me.'

Pontifex stares at the fiver. 'Dear child, this is most unexpected. How can I ever repay your kindness?'

'By getting out of here before someone notices that I'm talking to myself, and sends

62

for the little men in white coats to take me away.'

Pontifex raises his eyebrows. 'Little men in white coats?'

'Another colloquialism,' I say. 'Don't get drunk again.'

I don't think you *can* get drunk on a fiver, but I give him the warning anyway. Pontifex doesn't seem able to look after himself properly.

15

Christmas Eve is practically a rerun of yesterday. Dad makes my breakfast and drives me to the airfield. As he pulls into the parking area he says, 'I'll be a bit late tonight. There's a party on at the office.' Dad doesn't sound thrilled; he hates parties.

'How late?' I ask.

'I'm hoping I can get away by half seven.'

I peck Dad on the cheek. 'Festivity is a real hassle, isn't it?' I say.

During the five-minute wait for Mr Fairbrother, I wonder where Christmas went. It used to be the one thing I looked forward to that wasn't a letdown, a time when dreams came true. Now Christmas Eve is just another working day. Maybe Christmas is something you grow out of without noticing.

I'm not in a particularly Yuletide mood, but Mr Fairbrother is. He's still smiling, and he's stuck a piece of holly into the top of his balaclava.

'I've taken a gamble and invested in some new stock,' he says, amazed at his own daring.

The new stock is lava lamps. They're shaped

like space rockets and when they warm up, the gloop inside them crawls around like a giant, coloured amoeba. I have a hunch that they'll go down better with the punters than fibre-optic lamps did. (I don't count yesterday, which was a freak blip caused by Pontifex.)

I'm right; sales are brisk. Loads of people have come to the market to look for last-minute gifts, and lava lamps fit the bill – not too pricey and the right sort of naff. Mr Fairbrother grows cheerier and cheerier, and I'm afraid he's about to sprout a white beard and start saying, 'Ho, ho, ho!'

When my lunch break arrives, I'm more than ready for my bacon roll and tea. Joe's entered into the spirit of things: as well as the regular menu, he's selling mince pies and slices of fried Christmas pudding (don't knock it until you've tried it). I'm enjoying hanging round the van, because people turn up to it cold and miserable, and after the food and drink kick in, they get this warm, happy glow.

Then I have that feeling you get when someone's watching you – you know, kind of prickly like your skin can feel a stare? I scan the crowd, and spot a young guy looking at me. His face is familiar, but I can't remember from where. It's an angular face, with curly brown hair and ears that stick out a tad. His eyes are dark and soft, with thick, sweeping lashes.

He's embarrassed that I've clocked him. His cheeks turn pink and he takes a half-step towards me, then changes his mind and comes to a halt.

I'm curious, so I go over to him and say, 'Hello.'

'Hello,' he says.

'Have we met?'

The pink in his cheeks darkens to crimson. 'Um, yes,' he says. 'Wednesday night at Aardvarks?'

Placed him!

'You spilled your drink over me!' I say.

He looks down at his feet. 'Sorry about that,' he mumbles. 'You were a bit annoyed.'

'I was ballistic.'

'Oops!'

'Not with you, with some creep who was all over me.'

He cautiously raises his eyes. 'I'd be happy to pay your dry cleaning bill,' he says.

Well-mannered, hey?

'It's cool,' I say. 'It was my fault. I should've looked where I was going.'

The guy offers me his hand – aaw, sweet! 'Drew Chapman,' he says.

I take his hand and shake it. 'Lauren Hunter.'

Drew takes in my manky jeans, tatty trainers, old leather jacket, grey woollen bobble hat and says, 'You work here?'

'Yeah, but not full-time. I'm in Year Eleven at Forest Road Comp.'

'I go to Redway Sixth Form College. I

66

started in September,' says Drew. 'I'm searching for inspiration.'

I get a wire crossed. 'And you're hoping that your A-level courses will inspire you?' I say, thinking he must be some sort of nerd.

Drew laughs. 'No, I've come to the market searching for inspiration. Can I pick your brains?'

'Me?'

'Well, you're a girl and—'

'Thanks for noticing,' I say.

'Any bright ideas about what present I could buy for my sister?' says Drew. 'She's thirteen.'

Being a natural-born saleswoman, I say, 'How about a lava lamp?'

Drew mulls it over. 'Not bad,' he says. 'Where would I get one?'

'Follow me,' I say, and Drew follows.

'I've seen you at Aardvarks a couple of times,' he says. 'You were with your friend – the girl with the reddy-brown hair?'

I've been here before, so I know what's coming. To save time, I say, 'Her name's Jessica. She's the same age as me and no, she doesn't have a boyfriend right now, but I'd move fast because she won't stay single for long.'

Drew is fazed. 'I didn't—! I wasn't—! I'm not—!' he splutters.

'You're not what?'

'I'm not interested in your friend.'

67

'Then you deserve a certificate for being the first,' I say, sounding humpy.

'She's . . . not my type,' Drew says.

Something's going on here that I don't get. Is Drew hinting that he's gay?

'It takes all kinds,' I say.

'Variety is the spice of life.'

'And a watched clock never boils.'

We both laugh. It snaps a tension that I hadn't registered was there.

Drew chooses a green and orange lava lamp, and as I hand him the bag, he says, 'Will you be at Aardvarks again next week?'

'Don't know,' I say. 'I haven't made any plans.'

'Oh,' he says. 'Perhaps I'll see you there some time.'

'I'll wear something waterproof,' I say.

Drew smiles – great overbite! 'Bye,' he says.

I watch him walk into the crowd, and I can't help doing a shoulders-buns-legs number on him. He comes out as 7.5, which isn't half bad.

An elbow digs me in the ribs. The elbow has Mr Fairbrother attached to it. 'Aye, aye!' he says.

'Aye, aye what?' I say.

'That young feller seemed very taken with you.'

'Huh?'

'Cupid's at work, if you want my opinion.'

'Oh, pur-lease!' I say. 'I've had it up to here with angels!'

68

Cue an afternoon of stick from my employer. Honestly, you say five words to a boy and people have you drawing up a guest list for the wedding. Apart from anything else, I suspect that Drew is a nice guy, and you know about me and nice guys.

The market is open until eight tonight, but Mr Fairbrother says he can manage and lets me knock off at the usual time. I get my wages, another twenty-quid bonus, the bus, and I'm home by five.

The house is empty. I find a note from Mum in the kitchen.

Gone shopping with Sarah. Should be back at 7.

In her dreams! Shopping with Sarah is a nightmare. I went with her to buy shoes once – never again. After trying on twenty different pairs, she bought the ones she'd first chosen. Sarah's not that fussed about shoes, but she loves giving assistants the run-around.

So, I have two hours of blessed solitude. I can veg out in front of the TV without getting grief from the Brat because she wants to watch something else. I go upstairs, change into something slobby – and the doorbell rings.

I hurry down. I'm praying that it's not old Mrs Bowles from across the road. She's a sweetie, but she's an international-level yacker.

In the hall I hesitate, because I can see Pontifex through the pebbled glass in the front door.

There goes solitude!

16

I yank open the door and say, 'Have you lost your tiny mind? What d'you think you're doing, coming to the house like this?'

Pontifex looks pleased with himself; if he was a cat, he'd be purring. 'I thought congratulations were in order,' he says.

'Why?'

'You've taken an important step forward. I know how difficult it must have been, but you made your message clear. He won't be bothering you again.'

'Pontifex, what are you babbling about?' I say.

A cloud appears to gather in Pontifex's eyes. 'Er, what day is this?'

'Christmas Eve.'

'Oh dear!' says Pontifex. 'Dear, dear, dear!'

I thought he looked rough yesterday, but today he looks worse. His clothes are a mess, his shoes are caked with mud and the smell he's giving off isn't summer-meadow fresh.

'When did you last have a wash?' I say.

Pontifex rubs his chin. 'A wash? Let me see

now . . . well, what with one thing and another, I haven't been able to spare the time.'

And suddenly, I'm the one in the tiny-mind-loss situation, because I hear myself say, 'Come in. You need a bath.'

I didn't have a clue that I was going to say this, and Pontifex crosses the threshold before I can take it back.

'Many thanks, dear child,' he says.

I close the door. 'Pontifex,' I say, 'I haven't mentioned it before, but all this *dear child* stuff really gets on my nerves. It's so condescending! Just call me Lauren, OK?'

'My apologies.'

'Accepted.'

I bundle Pontifex up the stairs, run the bath and find him a towel. 'You have an hour,' I say. 'Put your clothes on the landing and I'll see what I can do with them. Don't touch the blue bath salts; they're Mum's and she throws a wobbler if anyone else uses them. One hour, understand?'

'Perfectly,' says Pontifex.

I make a discreet withdrawal while he undresses, then I pick up his clothes – suit, shirt, tie, shoes. Angels don't appear to need underwear or socks – which is good, because I wasn't looking forward to dealing with those. I take the clothes to the kitchen, put the shirt into the washing machine, scrub the shoes with an old newspaper and give the suit and tie a thorough sponge-down.

71

Whoa! If you're thinking that one day I'll make a tidy little housewife, think again! The only reason I'm doing these things is to get shot of Pontifex quickly. I'm laying my butt on the line for him because . . . because . . .

A voice begins to sing upstairs; high, pure and beautiful. I don't know the melody it's singing, but it reminds me of Christmas magic, snow on fir trees, frost ferns on window panes. If I peeked out of the kitchen window and saw Santa's sleigh parked on next door's roof, it wouldn't throw me. I'm blissed-out: bottle this feeling and it would be an illegal substance.

I'm still floating as water gurgles down the drainpipe and Pontifex strides into the kitchen, wrapped in Dad's towelling bathrobe.

'I hope it's all right for me to borrow this,' he says.

'Was that you singing?' I ask dreamily.

'Um, yes. Did I disturb you?'

There isn't a word for what the singing did to me. I'm so carried away, I forget about my rush for Pontifex to be somewhere else, and say, 'Can I get you something to eat?'

'That would be most generous of you,' Pontifex says.

I take him into the lounge, draw the curtains, switch on the TV and push him onto the sofa. He stares in fascination at the Christmas tree. 'What's that on top?' he enquires.

'An angel,' I say.

'*Really?*' says Pontifex. 'Isn't it rather—?'

72

I don't stay for the rest; the singing has worn off, and I'm aware of the time again. I scuttle to the kitchen, cobble together a cheese toastie, and pour a glass of milk. The washer is tumbling Pontifex's shirt dry. The arms of the shirt flap like wings as the drum revolves.

Back in the lounge, Pontifex takes the milk and toastie without removing his eyes from the TV. 'Tell me, Lauren,' he says. 'Do people actually find this kind of violence and mayhem entertaining?'

'No,' I say. 'You're watching the news.'

It's going well. I'm cool, calm and in command. In ten minutes, Pontifex will be gone. I'll clean the bathroom and remove all evidence of his visit. My family need never know that Pontifex was here, which is just how I'd like it. The worst scenario would be for someone to come home early and it won't happen, because not even *I* could be that unlucky – especially with my guardian angel at my side.

A key rattles in the front-door lock.

Dad's voice calls, 'Hello, it's me!'

17

Here comes a snazzy special-effects sequence. I move so fast that I split myself in two. One of me stays near the sofa; the other me crosses the room, trailing a stream of ghostly light, grabs the lounge door, closes it behind me and leans against it. 'Dad!' I say. 'You're not late. I thought you were going to be.'

'I managed to slip away,' says Dad.

I say the first thing that pops into my head. 'Is that wise? I mean, won't you be in trouble if the big boss notices that you're not there?'

'The state he was in when I left, he wouldn't notice I was missing if I was three metres tall with bright purple hair,' Dad says.

'Are you sure? Maybe you should go back to the office and sneak in for another half hour, just to be on the safe side.'

'No,' says Dad. 'I've had a lucky escape. All I want is a quiet evening in.'

There's not much hope of that, unless I can think of something. Please, brain, get me out of this!

'Is your mother about?' says Dad.

'She's taken Sarah shopping. They'll

probably be ages. You know what Sarah's like. She'll drag Mum round Principles, French Connection, Miss Selfridge, John Lewis—'

There are plenty more names on my list, but Dad cuts me short.

'Lauren,' he says, 'is everything all right?'

'Sure!' I say. 'Fine! Couldn't be better!'

'Who are you hiding in the lounge?'

'Nobody! Absolutely nobody! What makes you think that I'm hiding anyone in the lounge?'

'The way you're standing between me and the door.' Dad gives me his Father-Knows-All look and says, 'What's going on, Lauren?'

I say, 'Nothing. Guess what Mr Fairbrother's selling now. Lava lamps – can you believe that? The Nineteen Seventies are really back in fashion, aren't they? D'you know how many people I saw wearing loon pants today? At least twenty – or was it more like thirty? Isn't it strange how—?'

'Lauren,' says Dad, 'quit stalling and let me into the lounge, please.'

I step aside. 'Help yourself,' I say.

I'm down to my last hope, which is that Pontifex is an hallucination that only I can see. If I'm wrong, Dad's going to leave a fair-sized hole in the ceiling when he hits it.

Dad opens the door and goes into the lounge, with me right behind him.

I see it all in detail: the twinkling lights on the Christmas tree, the flickering of the TV;

75

Pontifex holding a glass of milk in his left hand, a toastie with a bite taken out of it in his right. He chews hurriedly, swallows and says, 'Good evening.'

'Good evening,' says Dad. Out of the side of his mouth he mutters, 'Who the hell is this?'

I say, 'Um, Dad, this is . . . Mr Pontifex. Mr Pontifex, this is my father.'

They nod at each other.

Dad says, 'Is that my bathrobe, Mr Pontifex?'

'It is,' says Pontifex. 'Lauren was kind enough to let me borrow it after my bath.'

'Bath?' says Dad.

Pontifex smiles. 'Perhaps I can explain.'

'I hope someone can!' Dad says.

Pontifex rearranges his face to look ashamed and humble. His voice is husky, like it's teetering on the edge of tears. 'This afternoon, I overindulged my weakness for alcohol, Mr Hunter. I wandered the streets in a drunken stupor, until I collapsed into the gutter outside your house.' Pontifex's eyes glisten. 'That's where your daughter found me. A less generous person would have contacted the police and had me taken away, but Lauren helped me to stand, took me into the house and cared for me.'

Pontifex's performance is so brilliant, it almost has *me* convinced that he's telling the truth.

76

'I see,' says Dad. 'Is there anyone we can ring to come and pick you up?'

Pontifex shakes his head. 'Not a soul. I have no friends, no family and no home.'

Dad takes my arm. 'Excuse us a moment, Mr Pontifex. I'd like to talk to Lauren in private.' He leads me into the hall and shuts the lounge door.

I say, 'Dad, I know I've been irresponsible, and I'm sorry. I'm an idiot for bringing a stranger into the house. He could've been a burglar or a homicidal maniac. I didn't think. It was a spur of the moment thing and – well, you've seen him. He's harmless, so—'

Dad gives me a big hug. 'I'm so proud of you!' he says.

'You are?'

Dad lets me go. His eyes are glowing and if I didn't know him better, I'd say that he'd had a glass too many at the office party. Dad's experiencing the Pontifex effect. He's as bewitched and bamboozled as the customers at the stall yesterday.

'Most people's charity extends as far as dropping a coin into a collection box,' he says. 'But you—'

Dad's about to come down with the gushes, which I could really do without, so I say, 'What are we going to do with him now, Dad?'

I'm terrified Dad will suggest that Pontifex spends Christmas with us, in a kind of do-gooding orgy, but he lets me off the hook.

'There's a Salvation Army hostel in town,' he says. 'They'll take care of him. I'll drive him there when he's ready to go.'

Dad's not thinking straight, but he believes he is and I'm glad.

Pontifex finishes his snack, goes up to the bathroom to dress and comes down. Dad doesn't comment on how a homeless, friendless person with no family comes to be wearing an expensive-looking suit (even if it does need pressing) and a classy silk tie.

Pontifex bids me a weepy farewell at the front door, but tips me a final wink to let me know that it's all an act.

The soundtrack breaks into busy music, and we have a series of jump-cuts: me attacking a ring of dirt in the bath tub with a sponge and a bottle of household cleaner; me putting away the sandwich toaster; me defluffing the washing machine; and me hoovering the trail of mud that runs from the hall to the bathroom.

I collapse onto the sofa, thirty seconds before Mum and Sarah arrive home, staggering under the weight of bulging carrier bags.

Mum looks whacked. 'I can't walk another step!' she wails. 'Lauren, be an angel and make me a cup of tea, would you?'

'I'll make the tea, but I'm no angel,' I say.

Sarah follows me into the kitchen. I can tell she wants to swank about what she's nagged Mum into buying for her, but instead she stops and sniffs. 'What's that smell?' she says.

'What's what smell?' I say.

'That smell I'm smelling.'

I test the air and there *is* a smell, sweet and heady.

'Have you been burning joss sticks?' says Sarah.

'It must be you,' I say. 'How many perfumes did you try on while you were in town?'

This satisfies Sarah, though it isn't her, of course – it's the scent of a newly-cleaned guardian angel.

A few minutes later Dad returns and I rush into the hall to greet him.

'Did it go all right?' I ask.

'Better than all right,' says Dad. 'I managed to slip away.'

'Excuse me?'

'From the office party. All I want is a quiet evening in.'

'What about the hostel?'

'Hostel?' says Dad. He hasn't the faintest idea what I'm talking about and I have a spooky feeling that I know what's happened.

I say, 'Dad, what's the last thing you remember?'

'You, asking me what the last thing I remember is,' says Dad. 'Why?'

'Just testing.'

Pontifex did this. He's wiped Dad's memory from when he came home earlier until now. That's scary! What other powers does Pontifex have, and how will he use them if he loses

79

control? He's already hit the bottle and neglected his personal appearance – does that mean that the rot has set in?

A chilling thought occurs to me. I'm not certain where Pontifex is from exactly, but I bet that it's not like here. This world is jam-packed with stuff you can indulge yourself in, stuff that Pontifex has never been exposed to before.

Who guards a guardian angel from temptation?

18

On Christmas Day, Mum and Dad rise at the crack of dawn to do lunch prep – turkey and all the trimmings. Dad rustles up his culinary masterpiece, scrambled eggs with smoked salmon, and calls Sarah and me down. After breakfast, we blitz the presents under the tree; everybody thanks everybody else. The Ladzcape CD is a winner, but unfortunately Sarah plays it, and the music is relentlessly cheerful. To avoid bloodshed, Dad makes Sarah wear headphones.

We wash and dress, then telephone far-flung relations, including Gran and Grandad (Mum's mum and dad) in Devon. When that's over with, Sarah whiles away an hour calling her mates to compare present notes. I don't remember my friends being that materialistic at her age but hey, we used to go around talking like the Teletubbies, so who am I to criticise?

At lunch we stuff ourselves, clear away and get psyched up for the traditional Christmas visit to our other Gran (Dad's mum) who lives in Maidenhead.

All morning I've been angsty, expecting

Pontifex to be around the next corner, or behind the next door, or to spring out of the loo while I was in the shower. Since he wasn't and he didn't, during the drive to Gran's I relax to the point of whimsy.

How do angels celebrate Christmas? Do they have a knees-up and get hammered on lager? Probably not. According to my research on the subject, there's this one bunch of angels who don't do anything but sing God's praises, twenty-four/seven. This leads me to some interesting thoughts concerning the size of God's inferiority complex, if he needs that kind of reassurance.

I think about these things to avoid wondering how Adam is spending Christmas. He has to be kept under lock and key for a while longer.

Gran gives us her usual cosy welcome. 'You've put on weight,' she tells Dad. 'You're looking tired, dear,' she says to Mum. 'It must be a strain, having a career and keeping the house tidy.'

It's my turn next. Gran looks me up and down, and says, 'You should let me put your hair up into a nice French pleat. I'm sure it would suit you.'

'I like my hair the way it is, Gran,' I say.

'Young people today are slaves to fashion, aren't they?' says Gran. Her face lights up when she looks at Sarah. 'Pretty as a picture! You take after me, you know.'

82

This is another fine example of faith in action, because there's no way that Sarah is anything like Gran.

'Sit yourselves down!' says Gran. 'You'll be wanting a bite to eat, I expect.'

'We've only just finished lunch, Mum,' Dad says. 'Don't go to any trouble.'

'It's no trouble.'

Gran wheels out an industrial-strength pork pie, a sherry trifle, a plate of cold ham, a Christmas cake, mince pies, pickled onions, pickled walnuts, pickled I-don't-know-what and I don't intend to investigate. Her dining room is a consumption camp.

'Did you have a turkey this year?' Mum asks Gran.

'It's too much bother for one,' says Gran. 'I had a poached egg on toast and that did me. Tuck in, everybody. Don't be shy.'

Duty-eating is tough, but if we don't get through it Gran will lay a guilt trip on us. When every mouth except hers is full, Gran says to Dad, 'Of course, Christmas was different when you were a child,' and proceeds to reel off stories that we've heard before – many, many times.

Poor Gran! She seems happier living in the past than the present. I ought to make the effort to see her more often, keep her company and—

Hold on, what *is* this? Am I turning into one of those caring, sharing type people? Hang out

83

with your guardian angel for long enough and it starts to rub off on you.

We leave Gran's at five.

In the car, I say, 'I feel sorry for Gran sometimes. She must be lonely on her own in that big house.'

'She won't be on her own much longer,' says Dad. 'Duncan's moving in with her after Christmas.'

'Good for him!' I say.

Sarah stiffens. 'Who's Duncan?'

'Gran's boyfriend,' says Dad.

'Gran has a *boyfriend?* Why didn't anybody tell me about him?'

'I just did,' says Dad. 'Anyhow, it's Gran's business, not ours.'

'Huh!' says Sarah. 'That's typical of this family. You hide the truth from me because you think I'm still a little kid.'

'Don't spit out your dummy, sis,' I say, which earns me one of Sarah's forest-fire glares.

Talk of Gran being on her own (or not, as the case may be) starts me thinking about Pontifex. I wonder where he is and what he's up to? He knows loads of stuff about me, although he doesn't always get it in the right order, but he doesn't know a whole lot about anything else. In fact, he seems to have trouble coping with being here. He's a refugee, an innocent who's been stranded in a wicked world.

84

In a funny sort of way, I feel responsible for him.

19

Next morning I wake up, think about what the day has in store, and it's not exactly a thrilling prospect. I'm not breathless with anticipation or anything.

The big disadvantage of Christmas Day falling on a Saturday is that Boxing Day is on Sunday, which means the shops won't be open again until Tuesday. This is particularly frustrating if, like me, a significant proportion of your presents have come in the form of money, tokens and vouchers.

There's not a lot to get up for, so I have a lie-in and do a quick review of my life, weighing up the pluses and minuses. On the minus side I have no boyfriend, a sister who's far better-looking than I am, a boring Saturday job and GCSE exams next summer. On the plus side I have Jess and . . . well Jess is pretty much it. I can't decide whether Pontifex counts as a plus or a minus.

Want a top tip? Whenever you have an urge to review your life, don't – it's way too depressing.

I haul my sorry behind out of bed and go

into the bathroom. Coming out, I see Sarah on the landing. She's got one of those plastic gizmos hooked over the top of her bedroom door, and she's hanging clothes on it.

'Gloating over the swag?' I say.

'No, I'm sorting out my new clothes,' says Sarah. 'These are the ones I'm taking back.'

I frown. 'Isn't that the skirt Mum gave you?'

'Uh-hu.'

'The skirt she bought when you went shopping on Christmas Eve?'

'Uh-hu.'

'Let me run this past myself one more time, sis. You picked out a skirt for Mum to buy you on Christmas Eve, and now you want to take it back?'

'Uh-hu.'

'You don't like it any more?'

'I love it!' says Sarah. 'But when I rang Cathy yesterday, she told me that Holly Stuart has exactly the same skirt. I'm not wearing anything that Holly Stuart wears – people would think I was copying her.'

'You worry too much about what people think,' I say. 'I don't give a stuff what anybody thinks of my clothes.'

'I know,' says Sarah, 'and it shows, doesn't it?'

Ah, the loving support of the family! What would I do without it?

I dress and go downstairs. Mum and Dad are getting to grips with a voice-activation package that Dad has bought for the computer. I know better than to disturb them; when technology and my parents collide, it's a struggle to the death.

I make myself tea and toast in the kitchen. My mobile is recharging on the work surface, next to the microwave. I've just got my toast nicely buttered and jammed, when the phone chirrups.

It's Jess. 'Hi, Lauren,' she says. 'You want to do something this afternoon?'

'What is there to do?' I say.

'Nothing, but it might be more fun if we do it together.' Jess lowers her voice. 'Can I come to your place? Richard is creeping me out.'

Richard is Jess's stepfather and there's nothing creepy about him, but he does that thing that stepfathers do – you know, when they try too hard because they want their step-children to like them?

'OK,' I say. 'What time?'

'Around two. I'll get Richard to give me a lift. Bye!'

Richard still has his uses then, creep or not. He's in a no-win situation with Jess. The more he spoils her, the more she despises him for it. Her problem is that her real father works in Saudi Arabia, and part of her is convinced that he took the job to get away from her. Her real father was the one who broke up the marriage and Jess is still angry about it, so she takes it out on Richard. I've told her that she isn't

88

being fair, but according to Jess it's Richard's fault – if he didn't want to be lumbered with a stroppy teenage girl, he shouldn't have married her mother.

This relationship stuff – who cares for whom, how much, when and why – is dead complicated, isn't it?

Lunch is cold turkey and a new concoction of Dad's – spicy fritters made from yesterday's leftovers.

Sarah prods the fritters with her fork. 'What are these?' she says.

'Fusion bubble-and-squeak,' says Dad. 'A delicious blend of organically-grown British vegetables, seasoned with choice Oriental spices and fried until golden. East meets West on a plate.'

Sarah impales a fritter, takes a microscopic nibble and pulls a face. 'It tastes gross!' she says.

'But it's vegetarian,' says Mum. 'Weren't you thinking of becoming a vegetarian?'

'That's kids' stuff!' Sarah says scornfully. 'Vegetarians are losers! Can I have the tomato sauce, please?'

Dad watches forlornly as Sarah smothers his creation in thick dollops of ketchup.

When Jess arrives, we do a bit of dolloping ourselves, because she's brought round a couple of face packs, a selection of skin-care products and a scented candle – all the right ingredients for a body-pampering session.

Before long we're up in my bedroom, listening to the stereo, plastered in gunk.

'Why was Richard bugging you?' I ask. I try to talk without moving my lips, so as not to crack the stuff on my face. (Mind you, I don't know why you're not supposed to crack it. Maybe the magic doesn't work if your skin is exposed to the air too soon.)

'He brought me breakfast in bed this morning,' says Jess. 'On a tray, with a flower in a little vase? The whole bit. He's so considerate it makes me want to scream!'

'I don't know how you stand it,' I say sarcastically.

'I put up with him for Mum's sake. Can we please talk about something else?'

'Such as?'

'Par-ty!' says Jess.

'When?'

'Tomorrow night. It's Sam Collard's birthday party. They've hired St Peter's church hall.'

'I thought you'd gone off Sam.'

'I have,' says Jess, 'but that doesn't stop me going to his party. You can come too.'

'I don't know if I should, Jess. Sam doesn't know me that well. I'd feel like I was intruding.'

This is an excuse. The real reason I'm reluctant to go is that I'm having a premonition that if I do, something awful will happen. I don't have a vision or hear the voice of Doom thundering in my ears; it's a mild sensation of

90

panic in the pit of my stomach and a tickle at the back of my neck. Could it be Pontifex giving me a warning?

'You're coming!' Jess says.

I know that tone of voice: Jess has just made my mind up for me.

20

Over the past week I've been giving belief a lot of thought, and the more I think about it the more confused I get, because people believe some *crucially* weird stuff. Like tonight: Sam's having a birthday party; it's what you're supposed to do on your birthday, right? People believe that birthdays are special occasions – but why? What are we celebrating, that we've survived another year? If survival is worth celebrating, how come we don't do it every day?

Another thing about birthdays is that you get older, which is nowhere near as straightforward as it sounds. Take me. I turned sixteen in September. I went to bed at night, forbidden by law to have full-on sex because I was too young, and when I woke up in the morning it was OK (well, not OK, but you know what I mean). What happened to me while I was asleep? If I underwent some mystical transformation, I wasn't aware of it. As far as I was concerned I was the same person that I'd been the day before. Is that nuts, or what?

Anyway, Monday begins like me – wrapped in a thick fog. There's been a frost overnight, and when I look out of my bedroom window, the back garden is white. It's like an illustration from a kids' book. Normally the back garden is just there and I don't pay it any attention; this morning the garden is different, all its ordinariness has become extraordinary.

Smack in the middle of my coming over all trippy-hippy, hello-trees-hello-sky, my premonition of disaster returns.

'Pontifex?' I say quietly. 'If you're available, I'd really like to talk to you about this.'

I wait for him to materialise in the room, but no dice. Me, have a guardian angel who appears on demand? You have to be kidding. I need a reality-transfusion to bring me back to earth, so I sling on some clothes and go downstairs.

I hear a voice in the lounge, take a peek, and Sarah is talking to the computer. Mum and Dad had no joy with the voice-activator, but Sarah has it sorted, no problem.

'This is excellent!' she says. 'The computer does whatever I tell it.'

'Yeah, I understand how that would appeal to you,' I say.

Sarah pokes out her tongue, then goes coy. 'You know that party you and Jess are going to tonight?'

'Y-e-e-s.'

'Would it be all right if I tagged along?'

'N-o-o.'

Sarah pouts. 'Why not?'

93

'Because everybody there will be older than you. You'd have no one to talk to.'

'I'd manage,' says Sarah. 'I prefer older boys. The boys in my year are so—'

'Like Year Nine boys?' I say. 'I've been there, and the answer is still no. Anyway, Mum and Dad wouldn't let you go.'

'Being fourteen sucks!' says Sarah.

I don't tell her that being sixteen also sucks; she'll find out soon enough.

The deal for the party is: rendezvous with Jess here at half seven; we walk to the church hall; walk back and Jess spends the night on a z-bed in my room. Mum and Dad have extended my deadline to eleven thirty (I tried for midnight but they beat me down) after delivering the routine no drugs, no booze, no hanky-panky lecture, which is kind of reassuring because it shows that they still care about me.

My preparations start at six, with a long bath and a hair wash. I dry my hair, put on make-up and choose my outfit. I go for something I can dance in, my aim being to look comfortable but classy. I miss, of course. When I inspect myself in the wardrobe mirror, it's still me. It always is, no matter how hard I try. The walk to the church hall will be cold, so I'm going to wear the coat with the outrageously-pink fun-fur collar that I bought during a momentary lapse in taste last winter.

Richard drops Jess off on the dot, and we head up the hill.

Jess has that look in her eyes, somewhere between a faun's and a velociraptor's. 'Are you ready to rock?' she says.

I say, 'No, but I'm prepared to sway from side to side a bit.'

'I'm up for this. I'm going to boogie the night away. Reckon we'll pull?'

'Haven't thought about it.'

Jess bumps me with her hip. 'Have faith, girlfriend!'

Faith again. It's easy for Jess to hold the unshakeable conviction that she's the most ravishing girl in the room, because generally she is. The best I can hope for is that the tragedy I *know* is about to happen won't include anything major, such as losing a limb or being forced on stage to sing along with a karaoke machine.

It's still foggy, but not as bad as this morning, and the church hall is like a little island of warmth and light. Sam's parents have done a thorough job. They've hired a bouncer to man the door, and provided him with a guest list so he can weed out would-be gate-crashers. My name isn't included on the list, which briefly causes embarrassment, but then Sam appears and clears me for entry. I think Sam was hovering near the door, waiting for Jess to show. He's certainly more pleased to see her than she is to see him. Jess gives him a birthday card that we've both signed, touches his cheek with her lips, and we swan in to the party proper.

Since it's a family do, a liberal sprinkling of adults is present, mostly seated at tables. This may be a church hall but it has a licensed bar, a DJ on stage and a laser-light display. Lots of kids are on the dance floor. Some of the boys are wearing dinner jackets and some of the girls are wearing long, satiny dresses; I feel severely outclassed.

Jess and I wave to people we know and – POW! Here's that disaster I've been expecting. A skyscraper collapses on top of me.

Adam is on the other side of the hall, in a white tuxedo with a red carnation in the lapel, and shiny-seamed black trousers. He looks positively edible.

My insides turn into mashed bananas.

'Jess!' I squeak. 'It's—!'

'Yeah, I knew he'd be here,' Jess says.

'And you didn't *tell* me?'

'Would you have come if I had?'

'No!'

'You can do this, Lauren,' says Jess. 'You're going to prove that you're over him. Adam Roden means nothing to you.'

I wish I shared her conviction.

For the next three hours, I throw myself into dancing. I smile and goof. Anybody watching me would figure that I was enjoying myself, and someone *is* watching me; Adam. I can feel

96

his eyes following me everywhere. I'm under siege. Memories I've been holding under bob to the surface and swim through my head – Adam's kiss, his smell, his arms around me.

At last it gets too much. I tell Jess that I need to cool down, and I go outside to the car park.

It's freezing. The mist has cleared, a half-full moon is up and there are more stars in the sky than I've ever seen before.

I have to let it all go: the sad dreams, the fantasies, the illusion of closeness.

A foot crunches on gravel behind me. I wheel around and whisper, 'Pontifex?'

Adam steps out of a shadow into the moonlight. 'How are you, Lauren?' he says.

'Good,' I say, though the real answer is that I'm emotionally bruised, battered and wrung-out.

'You look great.'

'You too. Nice jacket.'

Adam shoots the cuffs of the tuxedo. 'It's my Dad's,' he says. 'I like borrowing his clothes. It winds him up, you know?'

'Adam,' I say, 'what do you want?'

'To talk to you.'

'So talk.'

Adam scuffles his feet, runs his hand over his hair. 'I've been thinking about you all the time,' he says. 'I can't get you out of my mind. Those things I said to you before, at the market? I don't know what made me do that.

97

I shouldn't have. I've been meaning to call you for days, but . . .'

'You didn't,' I say.

'I wasn't sure how you'd react. I thought you might hate me or something. I wouldn't blame you if you did.'

'That's big of you.'

Adam writhes, like he's wrestling with himself. 'Are you going to give me a hard time with this?'

'With what?'

'What I'm trying to say.'

'And that would be?'

Adam lets it out in a rush. 'I want us to get back together.'

I can see his words, grey mist hanging on the cold air. I know this routine: he's giving it Soulful Adam, the sensitive boy who screws up without meaning to; he never makes mistakes, only miscalculations, and you have to forgive him because he's such a fluffy puppy dog.

'That's some ego you have there, Adam,' I say. 'Thanks for offering to share it with me, but I've had my turn. Go find another victim.'

Adam stretches out his hand. 'Lauren, I thought we had something.'

'We did. We don't any more.'

Adam doesn't get it. He drops his hand and says, 'I don't understand why you're being like this.'

I say, 'Because it's who I am now.'

Adam sees that it's true. I'm immune to him;

98

his charm, magnetism – whatever – won't work on me. He says, 'If you change your mind—'

'Sorry, Adam,' I say. 'I won't.'

Adam shrugs and goes back into the hall.

I've done it; I'm free. Do I cheer triumphantly and jump up and down? Get real! I'm trembling all over and I'm torn apart. The impulse to run after Adam is incredibly strong, but I have to resist it. I know this is absolutely the right thing for me to do, but why does it feel so lousy?

'Lauren?' Jess crosses the car park towards me, her eyes filled with concern. 'Lauren, are you OK?'

'I guess,' I say. I'm guessing that I guess, I don't actually know.

'I saw Adam follow you outside. Did he talk to you?'

'Yes.'

'What did he say?'

'He wanted to get back together. I told him no.'

'Well a-a-ll right!' Jess whoops. She grabs me, and dances me round the car park in a crazy waltz. 'Guys?' she yells. 'Who needs 'em?'

And at that moment, in the car park, dancing under the moon, *we* don't.

Jess and I leave soon after. There's a bottle of low-alcohol peach fizz in the fridge at home. I'm going to smuggle it up to my bedroom to toast the new, improved me.

99

Jess has her arm linked through mine, and gives me a squeeze. 'You are so cool!' she says. 'D'you give lessons?' Then she stops dead and stares. 'What the—?'

I look where she's looking.

About fifty metres ahead of us is a street lamp. Three guys are staggering in the light of the lamp and at first I think they must be drunk, but then I realise that they're fighting. It's two against one, and the one isn't doing too well.

'Hoi!' Jess shouts.

The two break off their attack and they're gone, streaking away into the dark.

The third guy crumples onto the pavement.

And I start running, because the guy on the pavement is Pontifex.

21

I'm frantic. I really don't want to look at Pontifex, but I have to, so I crouch down.

Pontifex is lying on his back with his eyes closed. His right eye is puffy and his top lip has ballooned up. I can't tell if he's breathing or what colour his face is, because of the orange lamplight. I'm scared and angry. How could anyone do this? Why would anybody want to hurt him?

I start to cry, partly for Pontifex, and partly for what happened between me and Adam in the church hall car park. My feelings have been put through a blender and they've turned out as tears.

'Pontifex?' I grizzle. 'Pontifex, say something! Speak to me!'

'You know him?' says Jess. She's standing behind me. I'd forgotten we were together.

'Kind of,' I say.

'Is he OK?' asks Jess.

She means is he alive, and I wish I could tell.

Pontifex twitches. His left eyelid flickers open; his right lid is swollen shut.

'Ah, Lauren!' he says. 'I was on my way to meet you.' He tries to raise himself on one elbow.

'Keep still!' I say. 'You might have internal injuries.'

Pontifex begins to smile, but the pain in his lip shrinks the smile into a wince. 'No need to be upset, I'm quite all right.'

'But your face!'

'Just give me a moment to recover.'

'Shall I call for an ambulance?' says Jess.

Pontifex holds up his hand. 'That's not necessary,' he says. 'I'm only winded.'

'Why did those two guys beat you up?' I say.

'They asked me for money,' says Pontifex. 'When I couldn't oblige them, they became agitated. Did I offend them in some way?'

'They were trying to mug you!'

Pontifex doesn't seem bothered about this, but something's troubling him. His forehead crinkles. 'There was something I had to tell you, Lauren,' he says. 'Something of vital importance . . .'

'Don't worry about it.'

I'm afraid it's my duty to worry about it. I might be able to think more clearly in a standing position.'

Between us, Jess and I haul Pontifex upright. He brushes dust off his raincoat and as he does, I notice that his eye and lip are back to normal. There isn't a mark on him and it's . . . well, miraculous.

Pontifex turns to Jess. 'You must be Jessica,' he says.

'Must I?' says Jess. 'I mean – yes, I am.'

'I'm delighted to meet you,' Pontifex says. 'You'll have two lovely children in the fullness of time.'

Jess can't say anything to this, so she just gawps.

Pontifex tugs the lobe of his ear. 'What *was* that message I had for you?' he says to me. 'Something to do with . . . a discovery . . . and—'

'Discovery?' I say.

Pontifex punches his left palm with his right fist. 'Eureka!' he cries. 'You mustn't give up.'

'I mustn't give up what?' I say.

'You mean you don't know? A pity, I was rather hoping that you would.'

Pontifex seems fine, but I'm still anxious about him. 'You've had a bad shock,' I say. 'Why don't you come back to the house, and I'll make you a mug of hot, sweet tea?'

'Appealing as that sounds, I'm afraid that I can't,' says Pontifex. 'I have an appointment to keep.'

'An appointment, at this time of night?'

Pontifex spreads his hands. 'Day and night are one to me,' he says. He carries on along Church Road; Jess and I turn onto Millbrook Close.

Jess hasn't spoken for a while, and I'm wondering if Pontifex has worked the same trick on her memory as he did on Dad's. She settles it for me by saying, 'Lauren who was that?'

'Pontifex,' I say. 'I must have mentioned him to you. I keep bumping into him. He's a bit shy, but he's very gentle. I think he may have a drink problem.'

'You've never mentioned him and you're not answering my question, you're trying to put me off,' Jess says sharply. 'Who is he?'

'It's a long story,' I say.

'I have loads of time.'

'And it's complicated.'

'I can do complicated.'

'You'll think I've gone psycho.'

Jess looks me in the eye. 'We're best mates, Lauren,' she says. 'Best mates trust and respect each other. If you don't want to tell me about Pontifex, I'm fine with it. I respect your privacy like you respect mine.'

I say, 'But if I don't tell you, you'll never talk to me again, right?'

'Right!' says Jess.

I gulp. On the soundtrack, the violins play a shivering, rising note that ends with the entire orchestra going – DA-DA-DA-DAH!

'He's my guardian angel,' I say. 'That's what he tells me, anyway. I think he believes it.'

'And do you believe it?'

Given all those thoughts about belief that I've been having, this is a tough call. If I say yes, it'll sound like I've flipped, and if I say no,

104

it'll be disloyal to Pontifex. So I grasp the Paper-Clip of Truth and bend it a little.

'I'm not sure,' I say. 'Sometimes I do, other times I don't.'

Jess says, 'I want the whole story, in detail, with action replays, starting now.'

The whole story lasts down the hill and into my house. There's a short interlude where I do some parental interaction, like – yeah, the party was a blast, but we're completely knackered, so we're off to bed. Then it's a lightning raid on the fridge to snaffle the bottle of peach fizz, and upstairs we go.

Even low-alcohol drinks have alcohol in them, and after a few swigs I'm pouring my heart out.

Jess listens to me ramble on, and when I'm done she says, 'So, either you're being stalked by a homeless con-man who uses hypnosis to give people amnesia, or you have an alcoholic, accident-prone guardian angel.'

'That's about it,' I say.

Jess sighs. 'Why can't you have ordinary problems, Lauren – like split ends and boy trouble?'

'I do, but I have Pontifex as well. Any suggestions?'

'Two,' says Jess. 'First, take a course in self-defence so you can flatten Pontifex if he tries anything on. Second, let's sleep on it. It might make more sense in the morning.'

We settle down and I turn out the bedroom light.

'Jess,' I say, 'what d'you think Pontifex meant about a discovery?'

'That's easy,' says Jess. 'You made a big discovery tonight.'

'Which is?'

'You can stand up for yourself.'

Jess is right, but there's more to it than that. What I discovered tonight is that I have a self worth standing up for.

22

Mum had to go back to work this morning, so at breakfast it's Dad, Sarah, Jess and me. Having Jess with us changes the atmosphere; she charms Dad's socks off, as per usual, and Sarah lightens up and drops the brat act.

Then Dad goes and puts his foot right in it. 'What's on the agenda for today, ladies?' he says.

'I'm going shopping with Jess,' I say.

Dad turns to Sarah. 'You want to take some clothes back, don't you?' 'Why don't the three of you go together?' Dad suggests.

Sarah and I both shout, 'No!' at once.

'I am not wasting an entire day traipsing round town with Sarah!' I snap.

'Dad,' says Sarah, 'you've seen the clothes that Lauren wears – what help would she be?'

'Sorry I spoke,' Dad mutters.

Jess smiles sympathetically. 'It's a generational thing, Mr H,' she says. 'You weren't to know.'

Jess and I make tracks straight after breakfast. Dad offers us a lift, but we tell him that we'd rather take the bus. On the ride into town

I don't mention Pontifex and neither does Jess, though I wish she would. What he said about not giving up is bugging me and I could do with talking it over. Did he mean don't give up on myself? Don't give up on the hope that somehow, somewhere, at some time there's a remote possibility that I might be happy?

It had to be me who got the absent-minded guardian angel, didn't it? It must have been like – oh, it's only Lauren! Pontifex will do for her.

That thought makes me feel guilty. Pontifex is doing his best. I'm sure he wouldn't get things mixed up if he could help it, but he can't – which is a shame. I'd better play safe and not give up anything.

Town is heaving with shopaholics suffering from withdrawal symptoms. The signs in the windows have changed from *CHRISTMAS SALES* to *JANUARY SALES*. Jess and I go to the Heron Reach Mall (which has no herons and doesn't reach anywhere, but they had to call it something) where we split up for a while. We do this because we value our friendship. Jess wants to buy a new lipstick, which will take her ages and would bore me to death; I've got a book token to exchange, and Jess has learned through bitter experience what that means.

I love bookshops, but as soon as I walk into one I become a total airhead. If I have a particular book in mind, I instantly forget about it and wander around looking at everything. This is probably why I can't stand shopping with Sarah – we're so alike, only with her it's clothes and with me it's books.

What am I in the mood for – crime, horror, a romantic weepie? On second thoughts, maybe not a romantic weepie; I've done enough romantic weeping recently, thanks. I climb the staircase to the Occult section on the first floor, to see if the shop has any books on angels.

It sure does! One book, *Angelic Hosts Proclaim*, weighs a ton and is 'lavishly illustrated' as the cover puts it. I flip through, checking out the pictures. None of them looks like Pontifex, but if you took a cherub, removed his wings, pumped him up to man-sized, dressed him in a suit and squinted at him sideways, he'd be Pontifex-ish.

I close the book, and there's Drew. He's standing in the Art section. He has his back to me, but I recognise his hair and green jacket (OK, I admit it, and his buns!). Don't ask me why, but I panic. If Drew spots me, I'll have to talk to him and if that happens . . . well I don't know and I don't want to find out. I leave before Drew can turn round and my timing is perfect, because Jess is about to come into the shop to find me.

'Did you get anything?' she says.

'No,' I say.

'Nothing you fancied?'

'Not really. Let's go to HMV.' I grab Jess's arm and pull her along.

'What's the rush, Lauren?'

The rush is, I don't want Drew to come out of the bookshop and bump into us.

'No rush,' I say, increasing speed.

In HMV I buy a couple of CDs, then Jess and I have a snack attack, so we go to Mambo. The decor in Mambo is wild and the menu is wilder. It's supposed to be Italian, but if you toss together a selection of the world's junk food, put it through a food processor and sling it into a warm ciabatta, you'll get the general idea – top latte though. We park ourselves on one of Mambo's two-person, bench-table affairs and I'm just about to plump for a ciabatta with chicken tikka masala and goat's cheese, when Drew walks in.

I think, 'Pontifex, you're my guardian angel – get guarding! Don't let him notice me!'

Drew notices me.

I think, 'Don't let him smile!'

Drew smiles.

I think, 'Don't let him come over!'

Drew comes over and says, 'Hi, Lauren.'

'Hi,' I say. 'Fancy running into you.'

'I had some shopping to do.'

'Then you came to the right place.'

Jess coughs to get my attention and raises one eyebrow.

'Oh, sorry!' I say. 'Jess, Drew. Drew, Jess.'

Drew says, 'Have you been shopping too?'

'Er, yes,' I say – like why else would we be in a shopping mall?

'Big place, isn't it?'

'Yes,' I say. 'Plenty of shops.'

Silence descends. No one's saying anything, but Drew is still standing there. The silence is on the point of becoming embarrassing, then Drew straightens his shoulders and says, 'Um, Lauren?'

'Yes?'

'Are you seeing anyone?'

And I am; I'm seeing him. There's this vulnerable look in his eyes, and he doesn't seem lost exactly, but something inside him is waiting to be found.

Jess loses patience. She stands up and says, 'Take my seat, Drew.'

'Sorry?' Drew says.

'Sit down!'

Drew sits.

Jess says, 'Drew, Lauren isn't seeing anybody but she's just been dumped, so watch out for a potential rebound situation. Lauren, Drew would like to ask you out. I'm going to sit over there.' She points at a nearby table. 'Shout if you need any help. Good luck, and be gentle with each other.'

Lauren leaves Drew and me alone together.

Drew laughs nervously. 'Jess doesn't hold back, does she?'

'You ought to hear her when she's direct,' I

say. 'Was she right – are you going to ask me out?'

'I'm working myself up to it. I saw you earlier on, in the bookshop? I followed you to HMV and then here.'

'You're joking!'

'No, I'm being honest,' says Drew. 'I nearly asked you out at the market on Christmas Eve, but I didn't think we knew each other well enough.'

'We don't know each other now!' I say.

'True, but if we let the chance go by, we never will.'

'And that would matter?'

'It would to me,' says Drew. He sighs and squirms. 'I'm making a mess of this, aren't I? This is so not like me. I'm not the impulsive type.'

I think I detect the run up to a classic come-on. 'Let me guess,' I say. 'You're a shy, sensitive soul who doesn't know how to act around girls.'

'No,' says Drew. 'I was in a serious relationship that lasted a year. I've dated a lot of girls since, but nothing long-term.'

'And I've just had my heart broken for the first time,' I say.

Drew nods. 'Bummer, isn't it?' he says.

I laugh. 'Yeah, as a matter of fact it is.' I recognise the signs of old hurt in him, places where he's still tender. 'Are you over it?' I say.

'What?'

'The serious relationship.'

112

Drew says, 'You don't get over stuff like that, you get on.'

He's being honest again and I like it; I may even like him but it's too soon to tell.

I say, 'So, ready to ask me out yet?'

'Just about,' says Drew. 'I'm going to a movie tomorrow night, and I'd like to see it with you. If you say no, I'll be deflated and have a bruised ego, but I'll live. If you say yes, I'll be—'

'Over the parrot?' I say.

'Sick as a moon,' says Drew.

And I feel us go – CLICK!

We chat for a few minutes, then Drew has to go because his parents are expecting him home for lunch. He's hardly out of his chair before Jess is in it.

'Did he ask you?' she says.

'Uh-hu.'

'Did you say yes? Tell me you said yes!'

'Yes, I said yes.'

'Knew you would!'

'How?'

Jess blinks at me like I'm Miss Dumb from Dumb Street, Dumbsville. 'Because he's lovely,' she says. 'No wonder you've been keeping him to yourself.'

'I haven't been keeping him anywhere!' I say. 'He spilled a drink over me at Aardvarks last week, I talked to him for about five minutes in the market on Christmas Eve, and that's it.'

'Aaw, how romantic!' says Jess.

'Jess, there's nothing romantic about having a drink spilled over you, or the market.'

'There is when you're with the right person,' Jess says.

I give up. If she wants to believe it's romantic, let her. But I have to confess, being asked out by Drew *has* made me feel better about myself – a tiny, tiny bit.

23

I'm back home by three, a little floaty because of Drew. I've never felt like this before.

When someone who goes to your school asks you for a date, you're seldom surprised. You've made quality eye-contact and scouts have been sent out to gather information. Then a mutual acquaintance casually mentions that so and so fancies you, and your reaction is reported back to whoever it is. So by the time it comes down to a one-on-one, you already know what will happen and what your answer will be – and so does the person asking, because no one wants to go through all that hassle to be turned down, do they?

But Drew was totally unexpected, like finding a tenner in the pocket of an old coat. Hey – somebody likes me, somebody thinks that I'm worth something! I try on the thought; it fits OK and feels pretty good.

Dad's been busy while I've been out. He's dusted, hoovered, stuck a load of washing on and now he's chilling in the lounge, watching an ice-hockey match on satellite TV.

'All shopped out?' he says.

'Mm,' I say.

'Buy anything interesting?'

'Mm.'

'Sarah's still out.'

'Mm.'

'Are you going to say anything other than *Mm*?'

'Sorry, Dad,' I say. 'I was thinking about something.'

This look comes into Dad's eyes. 'Actually, I'm glad we're alone. I've been wanting to have a word with you.' A serious word, by the sound of it.

'Oh?' I say.

'The other Sunday, when you announced that you were going to church, your mother and I were quite concerned. I know that belief is an intensely personal thing, and I don't mean to interfere, but is there something that you'd like to share with me?'

I know just what he's getting at. 'Relax, Dad,' I say. 'I'm not about to go happy-clappy on you. I needed to confirm that I am still an agnostic, and I am.'

I don't mention that I received the confirmation from an angel; I don't understand that part myself.

'And how's the broken heart?' Dad asks.

'On the mend,' I tell him.

I watch TV with Dad. I couldn't care less about ice-hockey and the rules are beyond me, but I stay because we've just shared a father-daughter moment that it would be a shame to ruin.

At four o'clock, events take a decidedly weird turn. A police car pulls up outside the house, a constable steps out, walks up the front path and rings the doorbell. Dad answers it. I turn down the volume on the TV and perch on the arm of the sofa so I can spy through the crack between the lounge door and its frame.

The policeman is chunky, twenty-something and seems unsure of himself.

'Would you be Mr Pontifex, sir?' he says.

Special-effects shot: my ears expand to five times their normal size and start flapping.

'No I wouldn't, Constable,' says Dad. 'I'd be Mr Hunter.'

'Ah!' says the policeman. 'You wouldn't happen to have a Mr Pontifex staying with you, would you, sir?'

'No.'

'I see,' says the policeman, sounding disappointed. 'Do you know of a Mr Pontifex living in this area?'

'I'm afraid not, Constable,' says Dad. 'What's this in connection with?'

The policeman sighs. 'To tell you the truth, sir, I wish I knew. I was checking through my notebook at the start of my shift, and I came across the name Pontifex and this address. Unfortunately, I have no recollection of making the entry. I thought that if I made some enquiries, it might come back to me.'

117

'I'm sure it will, Constable,' Dad says. 'I'm sorry I couldn't be of more assistance.'

'That's all right, sir,' says the policeman. 'Thanks for your time.'

Pontifex is in trouble with the law!! He's zapped the memory of a policeman, which counts as obstructing the course of justice, doesn't it? What is Pontifex playing at?

Guardian angels! If you take your eyes off them for a second, they get up to all sorts.

I worry about Pontifex, but I stop when Sarah comes in because she bores it out of me. She empties the contents of her carrier bags onto the lounge floor, and goes through the ins and outs of what she bought where, and why.

Finally, Dad's eyes glaze over. 'Well done, Sarah,' he says. 'But I think you should put all those things away now. Your mother will be home before long. Let's get dinner ready for her, shall we?'

'But I'm tired out!' Sarah grumbles.

'It doesn't take much energy to chop an onion,' says Dad.

Sarah flounces a blouse into a bag. 'What are we making?'

'A curry. It'll use up the last of the turkey.'

Sarah wrinkles her nose. 'If I eat another mouthful of turkey, I'll turn into one!'

I say, 'That explains the scraggy red neck.'

Sarah blows a raspberry.

'Can you make that noise with your mouth as well?' says Dad.

118

The evening meal goes smoothly. Sarah repeats her shopping monologue for Mum's benefit. Mum does that thing where she appears to be listening when she isn't, and when it's quiet she says, 'How about your day, Lauren – did anything exciting happen?'

'I went into town with Jess,' I say. 'She bought a lipstick, I bought some CDs, we had lunch in the mall.' I pause: one, two three. 'Oh, and a boy asked me for a date.'

'A boy?' says Sarah.

'Yeah, you know – one of those people who shave their faces but not their legs?'

'Asked you for a *date*?' says Sarah.

'Yes.'

'Did he look desperate?'

'Sarah!' Dad says sternly. 'Is this boy anyone we know, Lauren?'

Dad's probing to make sure that I haven't taken up with a gorilla who smokes crack.

'I don't think so,' I say. 'His name's Drew Chapman. He's in his first year at Redway Sixth Form College.'

'Where did you meet him?' says Mum, probing too.

'At Aardvarks, last week.'

'Huh!' says Sarah. 'You don't waste much time, do you? One minute you're pining for Adam, next minute you're with someone new.' She says this like she thinks I'm some kind of floozie. She's miffed because she wasn't the

119

first to know. I knew that she'd be miffed; that's why I didn't tell her.

'What's Drew like?' says Dad.

I say, 'He's got two of everything he should have, he's polite and he talks nicely, but not posh. Jess thinks he's lovely.'

My parents are relieved by this news – they trust Jess's judgement.

'And he wants to go out with you?' says Sarah. 'I'll never understand boys!'

She won't have to; in a year's time, boys will be forming a queue that will stretch from the front door to the end of the street.

Just for the moment, I've got the upper hand where boys are concerned. I'd better enjoy myself while I still can.

24

Jess rings me next morning.

'What are you wearing for the date with Drew tonight?' she says.

'Clothes,' I say.

'Yeah, but which clothes?'

'Give me a break will you, Jess? It's only ten thirty. My fashion-sense won't wake up for another hour.'

'You have to make a good impression.'

'Jess,' I say, 'Drew's seen me in my market clothes. Anything would make a better impression than that.'

Jess has a point though. I guess a first date is a lot like test driving a new car to see whether you like it or not. What I wear tonight is especially important because Drew and I hardly know each other. I could dress up as anybody: sophisticated woman-of-the-world, sweet sixteen, slob, tart (not a serious option). I begin to wonder how Drew prefers girls to dress; then I realise what I'm doing and stop.

'I'm going to wear something that makes me look like me,' I say. 'I had two months of dressing to please Adam, now I'm going to please myself.'

'So it's the Native American headdress, diamante thong and Doc Martens?' says Jess.

'Too formal.'

'Those bottle-green jeans suit you, and that top with the big buttons . . .'

By the time Jess has finished, she's planned out my entire ensemble, and it's exactly what I was going to choose.

The jitters start at four o'clock and get gradually worse. I don't know why I should be stressing over this date; I have nothing to lose except my self-esteem. To calm down, I get ready way too early and end up mooching around downstairs.

Dad's in the kitchen, consulting cookery books. 'You're pacing,' he says.

'Am I?'

'Take it easy.'

'But what if he stands me up, Dad?' I say. 'What if he was stringing me along? What if he can't make it for some reason?'

'What if he's there and you both have a great time?' says Dad.

I hadn't considered that; I was too busy with doom and disaster.

'Shall I make you a sandwich?' Dad says.

'No, I couldn't eat a thing. Save me some dinner. I'll microwave it when I get in.'

'You're not worried that your stomach might rumble?'

'OK, OK!' I say. 'I'll have a sandwich.'

While I'm eating, Sarah walks into the kitchen. 'Is he good-looking?' she says.

'Who?' I say.

'This Drew guy.'

'He's all right, I suppose. Jess thinks he's good-looking.'

'Then why is he taking you out instead of her?'

'Beats me, sis. Maybe he has no taste.'

'He has taste,' Dad says quietly.

'D'you reckon he's a good snogger?' says Sarah.

'How would I know?' I say. 'You want me to take notes or something?'

Sarah's needling me because she's jealous, and it's working.

Dad spots a row brewing and says, 'Sarah, why don't you get on-line with your friends? You can tell them about your new clothes.'

Sarah huffs, but goes away.

Dad says, 'I'll give you a lift into town.'

'So you can check Drew out? I don't think so!'

Dad shrugs. 'Oh well! It was worth a try.'

I catch the bus at six, figuring I'll settle my nerves with a stroll round town before I meet Drew at seven, and my luck maintains its customary high standard, because the bus gets snarled in this massive traffic jam. What do I do? Would it be quicker to walk? How long will Drew hang on for me?

123

The bus reaches the station at ten to seven. I hurry through the streets, twisting and turning to avoid colliding with people.

Drew is outside the cinema. He's wearing a dark brown brushed-cotton top with a turtle-neck. He looks soft and cuddly in it. He greets me with a smile.

I'm hot, flustered and out of breath. 'Bus!' I gasp. 'Traffic!'

'You're right on time,' Drew says.

'Had to run!'

'I didn't think you were panting because of me.'

We enter the cinema and join the queue for tickets.

'Which movie are we seeing?' I ask.

'*Silent Strangers*,' says Drew. 'Unless you'd rather see something else.'

As it's Christmas, most of the other movies on offer are spin-off TV cartoons.

'*Silent Strangers* is OK with me,' I say. 'It's a science-fiction movie, right? You keen on science fiction?'

'Mad for it,' says Drew. 'I'm a Trekkie. I spend entire weekends in my Klingon outfit.' He catches the expression on my face and laughs. 'Joke!' he says.

Phew!

The movie is one of those are-there-aliens-among-us type things, and is pretty gripping, but my attention wanders. Visitors from outer space remind me of Pontifex. What did he do

124

that rated a mention in a policeman's note-book? If he gets himself arrested, the media coverage will be mega. Will I get dragged in? If Pontifex has committed a crime, does it mean that I'm guilty of something too – like failing to exercise due care and attention whilst in possession of a heavenly being?

The final credits roll. Drew and I discuss the movie as we file out. He's noticed a lot of stuff that I didn't, so I mark him down as a possible movie-buff.

It's cold on the street. We've reached that dodgy point: if it hasn't worked out, we say goodbye, go home and leave it at that; if things seem promising, we'll find an excuse to extend the time together.

Drew says, 'Hot chocolate?'

'Excuse me?' I say.

'I could murder a hot chocolate – are you up for one?'

'Yeah!' I say. 'There's this coffee bar not far away. I used to go there with—'

Drew wags a finger at me. 'Ah-ah!' he says. 'All mention of exes is strictly forbidden, agreed?'

'Agreed. What subjects aren't forbidden?'

'Literature,' Drew says. 'I saw you in the bookshop yesterday, so you can read, yes?'

'As long as you let me use my finger and move my lips.'

'Who's your favourite author?'

'I have thousands of favourite authors.'

'Name one!' says Drew.

And we're away, chattering nineteen to the dozen. We're like old friends catching up after a long parting. Next thing I know we're in a café, with empty chocolate cups in front of us, and my deadline is looming.

'My bus leaves in ten minutes,' I say.

'Are we going to do this again?' says Drew.

'I'd like to.'

'Tomorrow?' says Drew.

'I'm not sure how I'm fixed for tomorrow. Give me a call?'

We exchange phone numbers.

Drew, walks me to my stop and when the bus comes in, he kisses me on the cheek and says, 'I was hoping I'd meet you, but I didn't know it was you until we met.'

Oh, wow! Do I feel some kind of wonderful or what?

The journey home isn't a bus ride, it's a voyage on a marshmallow cloud. In my mind I burst into song, the other passengers join in, and it's a big production number with chorus girls and guys in top hats and tail coats. Life is a West End musical, and I'm the star.

I almost miss my stop. I'm so late with the bell that the bus driver has to brake sharply, and he gives me a dirty look when I get off. I don't care; the orchestra is still playing in my head.

The music fades on Somerset Avenue. A huge, shiny, top-of-the-range German saloon car glides past and parks at the kerb, twenty metres in front of me. As I walk by, the passenger window slides down. The driver leans over and says, 'Going my way?'

I say, '*Pontifex?*'

25

Pontifex is different. He looks fuller somehow, sleeker and cleaner. He's wearing a new suit, and a thick gold identity bracelet dangles from his left wrist. There's an iffy air about him, kind of flashy and geezerish.

'I trust you had a pleasant evening?' he says.

'Never mind my evening,' I say. 'Whose car is this?'

'I don't know,' says Pontifex. 'I happened across it in a quiet street and borrowed it.'

'You mean you *stole* it?'

'Not at all. I intend to return it in due course.'

'Is that why the police are after you?'

'The police?'

I put my hands on my hips. 'A policeman came to the house yesterday. He was looking for you. What's the story, Pontifex?'

Pontifex wilts under my stony stare. 'I seem to have a vague recollection of talking to a police officer last night,' he says. 'The officer mentioned something about my being drunk and disorderly, and taking me into custody for

128

my own protection, but I persuaded him otherwise. We parted amicably.'

'That's because you messed with his head to make him forget, isn't it?'

'I may have,' says Pontifex.

He's wordy again and I know why. 'You're drunk again!' I say.

Pontifex beams at me. 'I've been celebrating my new prosperity.'

'What prosperity?'

'A friend of mine explained the fundamental principles of horse racing to me. He advanced me a modest sum, which I took to a betting shop. Fortune smiled on me.'

'Well of course Fortune smiled on you, you're an angel!' I say. 'Isn't gambling a sin?'

'Not in the strictest sense, though it's frowned upon in certain quarters.'

At this point, I become aware that we're not alone. Someone else is in the car. I squint through the open window and see a brassy-blonde woman passed out on the back seat. 'Who's she?' I ask.

'Sandra,' says Pontifex. 'We met in the foyer of the Shaftesbury Hotel. I'm currently staying there, in a top-floor suite.'

If he can afford a suite at the Shaftesbury, Fortune didn't just smile on Pontifex, it burst out laughing and handed him the jackpot.

'Why is she in the car?' I say.

'We're returning from an evening in the Vegas Sands Casino,' Pontifex declares proudly. 'Rather a successful evening, if I do say so myself.'

The Vegas Sands is near the railway station, and it's a bit of a local legend. The clientele is far from savoury and rumour has it that you can get anything there – including a knife between the shoulder blades.

'Stay well clear of that dive!' I warn Pontifex. 'A lot of the people who go there are crooks.'

'All the people I encountered were perfectly charming,' Pontifex says. He pats the passenger seat. 'May I drive you home?'

'No! How come you can drive, anyway? Who taught you?'

'I receive guidance.'

I don't think he's talking about a satellite navigation system.

'Are you sure that I can't give you a lift?' says Pontifex.

'Positive.'

'Then I shall be on my way.'

I say, 'Look, Pontifex, you're getting yourself mixed up in stuff you don't understand and you're putting yourself in danger. What kind of an example is that for a guardian angel to set?'

Pontifex shrugs. 'Your concern for my welfare is touching, but misplaced. I am, as I believe the colloquialism runs, having a ball.'

And he drives away before I can stop him. There's no time for me to consider what I should do. If I'm not home in three minutes,

I'll miss my deadline, and Mum and Dad will ground me. I can't afford to let that happen, because of Drew.

I sprint, reach a speed that would astound my PE teacher, and make it with ten seconds to spare.

Mum and Dad grill me about the date. I answer their questions without giving too much away. How I manage this I don't know, because my brain is spinning like a plate on top of a juggler's stick. Later, when I'm lying in bed with the light off, I take a crack at estimating how serious things are.

Pontifex is in deep doo-doo. He's borrowed a car without the owner's permission, driven it while under the influence of alcohol, he's gambling and has started mixing with criminals and loose women. (I don't actually know that Sandra is a loose woman, but what I saw of her more or less fits my mental picture of what a loose woman looks like.) He's becoming more worldly and self-indulgent by the second. If he carries on like this, he'll be totally corrupted – and what then? What happens to angels who turn bad? Satan and his mob are supposed to be fallen angels – is Pontifex going to turn into some sort of demon?

I wish I could turn this mess over to someone who knows what they're doing, but I can't.

Pontifex is *my* problem.

26

With the morning comes a rare moment of clarity. I don't have any answers to the Pontifex problem, but maybe I'll find one if I talk it over with somebody – like putting things into words might make them seem more straightforward. It would be ideal if I could come clean to Mum and Dad, but I don't think they'd understand. They'd connect it with my visit to St Peter's and conclude that I was suffering from religious mania. Sarah doesn't even make my last-person-on-earth list; which leaves Jess. Jess already knows about Pontifex and she's met him. The fact that she hasn't so much as mentioned his name since could mean that she'd prefer to pretend it didn't happen, but she's bound to lend me a sympathetic ear, and right now I could do with one.

I get up in positive mode. Enough of sitting back and letting things happen to me – time for action!

Drew is keen. I can tell, because he rings me just after I've finished breakfast.

'Hi, Lauren,' he says.

Hearing him speak my name makes me come over all gooey. 'Hi, Drew,' I say.

'Sorry for ringing so early, but I couldn't wait to talk to you any longer. Last night was—'

'Yeah, wasn't it?'

'You're so—'

'You too,' I say.

'Shall we—?'

'Definitely, but not today. I have to do a favour for a friend.'

'Oh!' Drew says, like I've spoiled his day. 'You're not playing hard to get are you?'

'As if! I'm not that sort of girl. Tomorrow's good. Meet me in the Mambo at one o'clock?'

'I'll be there.' Drew hesitates, as if he wants to tell me something but isn't sure whether he should. 'Lauren,' he says, 'about last night? Was it just me, or—?'

'It wasn't just you,' I say.

I put the phone down and catch Sarah ducking back into the lounge. I go after the little minx. 'Were you listening in just now?' I say.

'I couldn't help it, you were talking in your mushy voice,' says Sarah. 'I gathered it was lover-boy.'

'No, it was Drew.'

'What did he want?'

'Er, to talk to me? Not that it's any of your business. If you dare earwig one of my telephone calls again, I'll—'

'You'll what?'

133

'I'll tell the olds about you and Martin Mason.'

Sarah pales. 'You wouldn't!' she says.

'Try me!'

And if you're curious about Sarah and Martin Mason, well tough! That's between me and my kid sis.

The phone rings. I get it, and it's Jess.

'I was just going to call you,' I say.

'Beat you to it,' says Jess. 'How was last night?'

She wants the uncut version, but I'm going to have to disappoint her. 'Jess, can I come over for a chat?' I say.

'What's the matter? Drew didn't stand you up did he?'

'I'll explain when I see you.'

'Will it involve crying?'

'No,' I say. 'I need your advice.'

'That bad, huh?' Jess says.

Since getting to Jess's means going into town and changing buses, I search out Dad. He's in the greenhouse, doing things with seed trays and a bag of compost.

I say, 'Dad, could you give me a lift to Jess's?'

'Yes, I *could*,' says Dad. 'I *could* stop in the middle of what I'm doing, this minute, and drive you to Jess's house, and risk road-rage while polluting the air with exhaust fumes.'

He's cranky, but it's no sweat. I lower my head and turn up my eyes. 'Will you – please?' I say.

Dad makes this noise that's part sigh, part growl. 'All right!'

'Cheers, Dad, you're the best! Have I ever told you that you look pretty good for a guy your age?'

'Only when you wanted me to raise your allowance,' Dad says. 'Lauren, I've agreed to take you to Jess's. Please don't butter me up any more, my stomach couldn't stand it.'

Dad goes into the house to wash his hands. I grab my coat, my purse and my mobile. We get into the car and set off.

'What A-level subjects is Drew studying?' Dad asks, trying to make it sound like an idle question.

'No idea,' I say. 'We didn't get round to stuff like that.'

'What stuff did you get round to?'

'Dad, we've been out together once! What did you get up to with girls when you were on a first date with them?'

Is Dad blushing? His ears are certainly red.

'Tell me one thing, and I promise to leave it,' he says. 'If you were to introduce Drew to your mother and me, would we approve of him?'

'Yes,' I say.

'That's all, just yes, no qualifications?'

'No.'

Dad smiles. 'That's my girl!' he says.

Dad drops me outside Jess's. I walk up the drive and ring the bell.

When Jess's mum opens the door, she lets out a blast of dance music that sets my back teeth buzzing.

'Hello, Mrs Bird,' I say. 'Is Jess in?'

Mrs Bird scowls. 'Yes, that's where the noise is coming from,' she says. 'Would you mind asking her to turn down the volume? I tried ten minutes ago, but I couldn't make myself heard.'

I go upstairs. Jess is in her bedroom, bopping in front of the mirror on her dressing table, watching the reflection of her wiggling butt. She throws her arms wide in a showbiz hello and kisses the air on either side of my face.

'Turn it down!' I yell.

'Sorry?' says Jess. 'Hang on, I'll turn down the stereo.'

The relief is blissful.

Jess sits cross-legged at the head of her bed; I sit cross-legged at the foot.

'So what went wrong with Drew?' Jess says.

'Nothing. I didn't come here to talk about Drew.'

'You didn't?'

'It's Pontifex.'

The corners of Jess's mouth droop. 'Ah, as in guardian angel Pontifex?'

'That's the guy.' I spill the lot: the car, the drink-driving, the nobbled cop, the Vegas Sands, the brassy blonde and the fate that awaits fallen angels.

'You mean this, don't you?' says Jess.

136

'Yes.'

'It's not some routine you're pulling on me as a practical joke?'

'Would I?' I say.

'No, and it's a shame. It would've made life less complicated. You know what you have to do, don't you?'

'No.'

'You have to talk Pontifex into going back.'

I'm not up to speed. 'Go back where?' I say.

'To where he came from,' says Jess. 'He doesn't belong here, and if what you've been telling me is true, the sooner he leaves, the better.'

Insert cliché of choice about Jess hitting nails on heads and putting things in nutshells.

There follows a sequence of shots taken with a hand-held camera, so the picture jerks and bounces. I leave Jess's house with a determined expression on my face, like here's a girl who knows what she's about. I take a bus into town, get off and march straight to the Shaftesbury Hotel.

I'm not looking so determined as I mount the steps that lead to the revolving door in the entrance. The Shaftesbury is a classy joint, well out of my league, and I'm afraid that someone will accuse me of trespassing.

There's a porter outside the entrance, wearing a blue uniform studded with brass buttons. He touches the peak of his cap and

137

says, 'Good morning, miss. May I be of assistance?'

'A friend of mine is staying here,' I say.

The porter says, 'Ask at reception. It's on the left as you go in.'

I pass through the revolving door, and enter Weird Central.

The Shaftesbury has been decorated in Ancient Egyptian style. Facing me is a giant plastic mummy wearing a gold death-mask, and in its hands is a tank of tropical fish. The walls are covered with hieroglyphic friezes and blown-up photographs of the Pyramids, and there are potted palms in every corner. Do people come to this place for accommodation, or to be entombed?

I have no trouble locating reception, because the big sign that says *RECEPTION* is a bit of a giveaway. I approach the desk. It's impossible for me to judge how long it took the receptionist to apply her make-up, but I guess she must have to remove it with a blow-lamp and a chisel.

'Good morning,' she says. 'How may I help you?'

'I believe a Mr Pontifex has taken a top-floor suite?' I say. 'Could you please ring him and tell him that Lauren Hunter would like to see him?'

'Certainly,' says the receptionist. She picks up a phone, presses buttons, waits, then replaces the receiver. 'There's no answer,' she says. 'Let me check for you.' She clatters the keys of a computer, glances at the monitor and says, 'I'm terribly sorry, but Mr Pontifex checked out early this morning.'

'Did he leave a forwarding address?' I say.

The receptionist smiles at me like I'm some yokel who'll never hack it in the big city. 'It's the hotel's policy not to divulge the personal details of its guests,' she says.

Well thanks for nothing!

I leave the Shaftesbury in despair. Pontifex could be any place. He urgently needs my help, but how can I help him when I don't know where to find him?

Another top tip: if some guy should turn up and say that he's your guardian angel, don't walk away from him – run!

27

Days go by with no sign of Pontifex and I stop fretting. I figure maybe he completed his mission, like he was a sort of Cupid who got me and Drew together and that was it. More days go by and suddenly it's back to school, and I haven't got time to think about anything except coursework, deadlines and yada-yada.

Drew and I chug along nicely. Each date is a different kind of special and we're definitely headed for falling in love without actually being there yet, which is good because there's something for us to look forward to.

January ends in two inches of snow that brings the country to a standstill. People are like, 'What, *snow?!* In *winter?!* Whatever next?!' and then nothing much else happens until Valentine's Day, when everything happens at once.

First off, I get two Valentine cards. One is from Drew, and I'm relieved that it's not one of those cute, blue teddy-bear type cards. On the front is a cartoon man and his face is bright red as if he's blushing, and inside it says, *I'll be thinking about you all day.*

The second card is yeuk! It has violet roses,

and lace, and gold, and I wish I hadn't eaten two pieces of toast for breakfast because it makes me want to puke. I open it, and then close it and stuff it back into its envelope as quickly as I can. I do this because in the card is a fifty-pound note and a message that reads, *Sorry for any inconvenience, P.*'

Now, I know that P stands for Pontifex but my parents don't, and they may well develop an unhealthy interest in why a strange man would send me money inside a Valentine card. Luckily they don't notice; they're too busy watching Sarah.

I have to admit, watching Sarah is kind of fascinating, in an appalling sort of way. She has a huge wodge of cards and she rips them open one by one, rolls her eyes, sighs, says, 'Oh, him!' and drops them into the wastepaper bin at her feet. She catches my eye and says, 'Why is it always losers who send cards on Valentine's Day?'

'Because nice guys try too hard,' I say.

Sarah puts on her nosey face. 'Two cards, huh?' she says. 'One must be Drew, who's the other one from?'

'No idea! Nobody. No one you know,' I say. 'It's this guy I've known for ages – well, we don't know each other that well, actually. It's a joke. He must have sent it for a laugh.' I'm making way too many excuses, and my family is staring at me. 'Look at the time!' I say. 'I'll be late for school if I don't get my skates on.'

141

I dive out of the room, just at the point where my family stops staring at me and starts staring at one another instead.

Later on, at break time, I shut myself in a cubicle in the girls' loos and take a closer look at Pontifex's card. The envelope has a London postmark, so I guess that's where he is – Temptation Central. His handwriting, if it is his handwriting, is like a little kid's, clumsily printed in lower-case letters. Angels don't seem to go in for joined-up. Are there schools for angels, and do they have to take exams? If they do, I don't think Pontifex got very good grades, and I wonder what happens to angels who flunk.

I put my questions on hold. The one solid fact I know is that Pontifex is still around somewhere or other. Two solid facts: he can also afford to give me fifty quid. A question slips under the locked door in my mind and expands until it fills my head. Where did Pontifex get the money?

This engages me for the rest of the school day, like my body turns up to lessons but I'm not really present. The last time I saw Pontifex he was gambling, and if he still is, that's where the fifty-pound note probably came from. There's nothing shady about gambling – well, up to a point anyway. Millions of people gamble, but I can't help feeling that Pontifex's angelic status gives him a bit of an unfair advantage, which means that he obtained the money dishonestly. I also can't help suspecting that there might be more to it than that because we're talking Pontifex, and nothing he does turns out to be straightforward. Whatever, there's not a lot I can do about it. I don't have his address so I can't return the money. Maybe I should donate it to a charity. The Samaritans would be appropriate, all things considered. On the other hand, perhaps Pontifex got himself a job and earned the money on the up-and-up, and fifty quid is fifty quid, the kind of sum that always comes in handy.

I've been placed in a moral dilemma by my guardian angel. Does that suck, or what?

At the end of school I go home with a lot on my mind. Mum and Dad are still at work, but the sound of the telly tells me that Sarah is in. I duck my head round the lounge door and say, 'What you watching?'

'Movie,' Sarah says.

'Any good?'

'Better than the rest of what's on. It's a who-dunnit.'

'And who did it?'

'A man with a moustache.'

'Wouldn't it have been quicker if he'd used a gun?'

Sarah peels her eyes off the screen and looks at me. 'You're weird,' she says. 'My sister, the weirdo.'

'Funny,' I say, 'I was just thinking the same thing.'

I go up to my bedroom and get changed. The collective noun for homework is 'a grind' and tonight I have an entire millstone to get through, but I'm too preoccupied with Pontifex to be able to concentrate properly.

The phone rings and a couple of seconds later Sarah yells, 'Lauren? It's Drew.'

I rush down and pick up the receiver. The daily paper's been left on the phone table, and while I talk to Drew my fingers fiddle with it. 'Hi!' I say. 'What's up?'

'Nothing,' says Drew. 'I wanted to wish you happy Valentine's Day.'

'Thanks for the card.'

'Thanks for yours. It was rude.'

'It was not! It was mildly suggestive.'

'Isn't that a biscuit?' says Drew.

I groan.

Drew says, 'Want to go clubbing on Friday? There's a new place opening—'

I glance idly at the newspaper, because I've ripped a long strip off one edge and wrapped it round my finger like a bandage, and the idle glance becomes a bug-eyed stare.

There's a picture of Pontifex on the front page. It's one of those photo-fit things, but it's close enough to leave me with no doubt. I scan the caption and words leap out at me: *wanted for questioning . . . failed attempt to rob a sub post-office . . . driver of the getaway car.*

I say, 'Drew! Sorry, can I get back to you later? There's something I have to do.'

144

I hang up. No lie; I do have to do something, and I wish that I knew what it was.

I wander into the lounge as Sarah lets out a cynical laugh. My paranoia instantly assumes that she knows everything about Pontifex, and I say, 'What?'

'This movie is dead corny!' Sarah says. 'I mean, that would so not happen in real life.'

'What wouldn't?'

'The murderer revisiting the scene of the crime.'

Freeze-frame: close-up of my wide eyes; sound effects of my brain going – DOING! ZIP! WHEE!

'That's brilliant!' I gasp. 'That's absolutely brilliant, Sarah! I ought to give you a great big soppy kiss.'

'You are *so* pervy!' Sarah says, horrified.

'I'm going out. Tell Mum and Dad not to worry if I'm late for dinner.'

'Where are you going?'

'To revisit the scene of the crime.'

Sarah frowns.

'It's a colloquialism,' I tell her.

She frowns harder.

I take a walk down by the river. The light is fading; the air, the sky and the water are the same shade of grey. There's no one else around except two kids riding bikes up and down a grassy slope, and once I round the next bend in the path, I'll be behind a clump of willow trees and they won't be able to see me.

145

I reach the university boat house, walk the length of the jetty and stand on the end. Then – and I know this is crazy but I have to follow my hunch – I take a deep breath and hold it in.

And I jump off the edge.

28

Do the icy cold arms of the river clutch me to its watery bosom? Does my past life flash before my eyes?

Nope.

There's a splash that's more like a KER-SPLUD, and then I'm standing in water up to my knees. My shoes are sinking into icky gunk and when I move my left foot, this revolting stench comes out of the river and goes straight up my nostrils.

Take it from me, you haven't appreciated just how moist water can be until you've stood knee-deep in a river on a cold February afternoon.

I squidge around, but all I succeed in doing is working my feet further down into the mud so that the water rises to my thighs. There's no denying the fact that I'm stuck, or that I'm a total dipstick. I'd cry for help to the two kids on bikes, but if they rush to my rescue they'll probably pee their pants laughing.

A familiar voice says, 'Oh dear, Lauren! What have you done?'

I twist round as far as the mud allows, and

I see Pontifex. He's on the jetty, gazing at me and sorrowfully shaking his head.

'Don't just stand there, Mr Guardian Angel!' I snarl. 'Help me out!'

I won't describe the undignified scene that follows, but it involves grunts, groans, a wet butt (mine) and an incredible sucking sound. Finally I'm back on the jetty, stinking and dripping and not best pleased.

'You knew the river was shallow didn't you, Pontifex?' I shout. 'You knew I wouldn't be able to drown myself that night you first showed up! You're a cheat!'

'I answered the call of someone in distress,' Pontifex says.

'If you think I was distressed then, what d'you think I am now?' I say, pointing to my soggy lower half.

'Wet,' says Pontifex.

'I've ruined my best jeans because of you!'

'Because of me?'

'Yes. I wanted you to appear, and chucking myself in the river was the only way I could make it happen.'

Pontifex blinks, nonplussed. 'You thought that I—?' he says. 'Because you—?' And he bursts out laughing.

I am *this* close to freaking. 'I'm glad one of us thinks it's funny!' I say.

Pontifex controls himself. 'I do apologise, Lauren, but it is rather amusing. My appearance has nothing to do with your . . . er . . .

aquatic escapade. I found you because I have something to tell you.'

'So I got soaked for nothing? Well that's great!'

Pontifex says, 'I've come to say goodbye.'

My anger instantly shuts down. I stop being Miss Sulky and start noticing things. Pontifex is wearing his old clothes; the flash suit and identity bracelet have gone. He's as sober and anonymous-looking as when I first saw him.

'You're leaving?' I say.

'I've received a summons.'

For a sec I think Pontifex is talking about a court summons; then the penny drops. I say, 'A summons from—?'

'Yes,' says Pontifex.

'I'm not surprised, after you got mixed up in an attempted robbery.'

Pontifex looks shame-faced and clears his throat. 'Ah, that!' he says. 'I was completely taken in by a man I met in a betting shop. He asked me for a lift to the post office so that he could purchase some stamps. I had no idea of his real intentions. People can be rather deceitful, can't they?'

'There's a lot of it about,' I say. 'I've been worried about you, Pontifex. Let's face it, this world isn't good for you.'

'You may well be right, but that's not the reason I've been summoned,' says Pontifex. 'My work here is done.'

149

'Work – what work? You haven't done anything!'

'It isn't what I've done, Lauren, it's what you've done,' says Pontifex. 'You've been caring for me since the moment I arrived, and it's changed you. Take a moment to reflect on what you've learned since we met.'

Hmm, what *have* I learned? Who was I before Pontifex came along?

I say, 'I didn't used to like myself much. I didn't believe I was lovable. I mean, I knew Mum and Dad loved me, but they sort of have to. I wasn't sure that anyone else would. For a while I conned myself that Adam did, but he just used me so he could love himself. I should have seen through him and fought against him, but I didn't know how.'

'And now?' says Pontifex.

'I've kind of grown on me,' I say. 'I'm more confident; I've found Drew—'

'You've found yourself,' says Pontifex.

This is heavy, heavy stuff.

'I guess that's down to you,' I say.

Pontifex smiles. 'It would be hypocritical of me to take the credit that rightly belongs to you,' he says. 'Feeling responsible for me has taught you to take responsibility for other matters.'

'Pontifex, are you trying to tell me that I've done a bit of growing up?'

'I prefer to call it development,' says Pontifex.

His goodbye is getting close; there's a sort of sadness between us.

'Any last words of advice?' I say.

Pontifex scratches his nose. 'Not as such, although it would be as well for you to bear in mind that Drew may not be the person whom you'll eventually—'

'I know,' I say. 'I have a lot of frogs to kiss.'

'Frogs?'

'Forget it.'

Pontifex thrusts his hands into the pockets of his raincoat, hunches his shoulders and says, 'I've become very fond of you.'

'Likewise,' I say. 'Take care.'

'I do little else.'

'No, I mean take care of you, not me.'

'I shall.'

'Will we meet again?'

'Who knows?' says Pontifex, glancing at the sky. 'These things move in a mysterious way. Farewell, Lauren.'

I say, 'See you, Pontifex.'

In the movie, we'd get some computer-enhanced trickery here, so that Pontifex fades to nothing, or soars into the heavens on a beam of golden light. In reality, he just walks down the path, away from the town, towards open fields.

As I watch him go, I think of something else that I've learned. Happiness isn't something that drops into your lap, it's something you have to work at, and a lot of it has to do with

151

the way you feel about you. You have to value yourself before other people can value you. This may not be the most original thought in the history of human philosophy, but it's mine and I'm going to cherish it.

My teeth are chattering. I have numb feet and my jeans are sticking to my legs. I can still see Pontifex, but to be honest it isn't that interesting watching someone walk away from you, even if he is your guardian angel.

I turn my back on Pontifex and head for home.

G.S.O.H.

'Thirty-something female, attractive, vivacious, WLTM male of similar age with GSOH.'

Fifteen-year old Katie is trying to get a date. Not for herself, you understand, but for her mum who, frankly, needs a bit of a helping hand. The thing is — once you start matchmaking you can't stop. What with Max, Briony, Jasmine and Dave to think about, Katie's got to get to grips with love in a big way.

ISBN 0099413892
£3.99